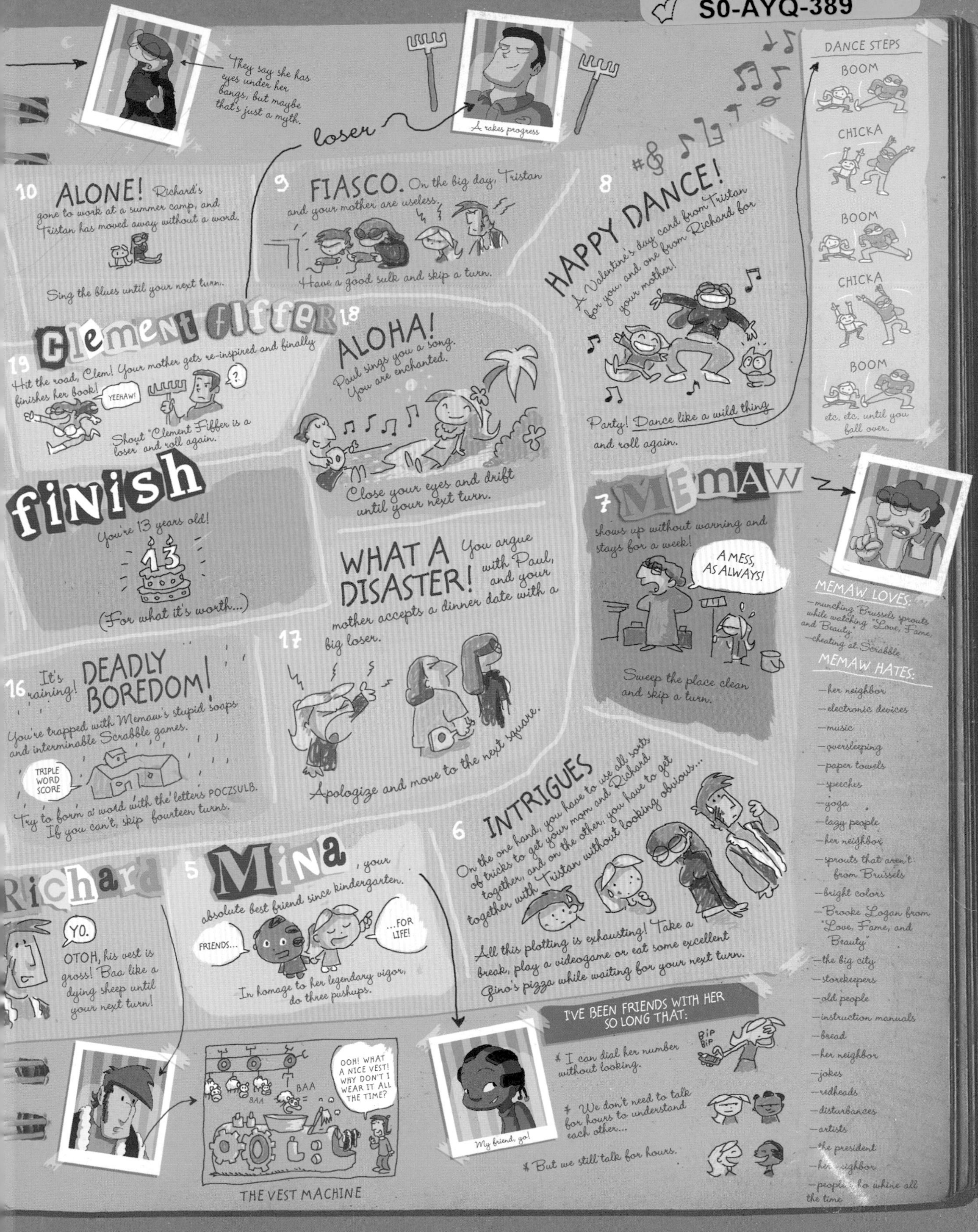

They say she has eyes under her bangs, but maybe that's just a myth.
loser
A rakes progress
DANCE STEPS
BOOM
CHICKA
BOOM
CHICKA
BOOM
etc. etc. until you fall over.
10 ALONE! Richard's gone to work at a summer camp, and Tristan has moved away without a word.
Sing the blues until your next turn.
9 FIASCO. On the big day, Tristan and your mother are useless.
Have a good sulk and skip a turn.
8 HAPPY DANCE! A Valentine's day card from Tristan for you, and one from Richard for your mother!
Party! Dance like a wild thing and roll again.
Clement Fiffer
19 Hit the road, Clem! Your mother gets re-inspired and finally finishes her book!
YEEHAW!
?
Shout "Clement Fiffer is a loser" and roll again.
18 ALOHA! Paul sings you a song. You are enchanted.
Close your eyes and drift until your next turn.
finish
You're 13 years old!
13
(For what it's worth...)
7 MEMAW shows up without warning and stays for a week!
A MESS, AS ALWAYS!
Sweep the place clean and skip a turn.
MEMAW LOVES:
—munching Brussels sprouts while watching "Love, Fame, and Beauty"
—cheating at Scrabble
MEMAW HATES:
—her neighbor
—electronic devices
—music
—oversleeping
—paper towels
—speeches
—yoga
—lazy people
—her neighbor
—sprouts that aren't from Brussels
—bright colors
—Brooke Logan from "Love, Fame, and Beauty"
—the big city
—storekeepers
—old people
—instruction manuals
—bread
—her neighbor
—jokes
—redheads
—disturbances
—artists
—the president
—her neighbor
—people who whine all the time
17 WHAT A DISASTER! You argue with Paul, and your mother accepts a dinner date with a big loser.
Apologize and move to the next square.
16 It's raining! DEADLY BOREDOM! You're trapped with Memaw's stupid soaps and interminable Scrabble games.
TRIPLE WORD SCORE
Try to form a word with the letters POCZSULB. If you can't, skip fourteen turns.
6 INTRIGUES On the one hand, you have to use all sorts of tricks to get your mom and Richard together, and on the other, you have to get together with Tristan without looking obvious...
All this plotting is exhausting! Take a break, play a videogame or eat some excellent Gino's pizza while waiting for your next turn.
Richard
YO.
OTOH, his vest is gross! Baa like a dying sheep until your next turn!
5 Mina, your absolute best friend since kindergarten.
FRIENDS...
...FOR LIFE!
In homage to her legendary vigor, do three pushups.
BAA
BAA
OOH! WHAT A NICE VEST! WHY DON'T I WEAR IT ALL THE TIME?
THE VEST MACHINE
My friend, yo!
I'VE BEEN FRIENDS WITH HER SO LONG THAT:
* I can dial her number without looking.
BIP BIP
* We don't need to talk for hours to understand each other...
* But we still talk for hours.

LOU! 3

Down in the Dumps

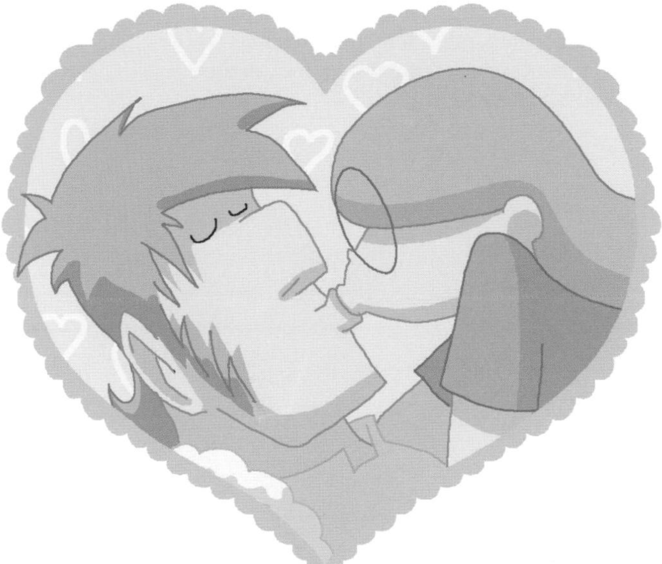

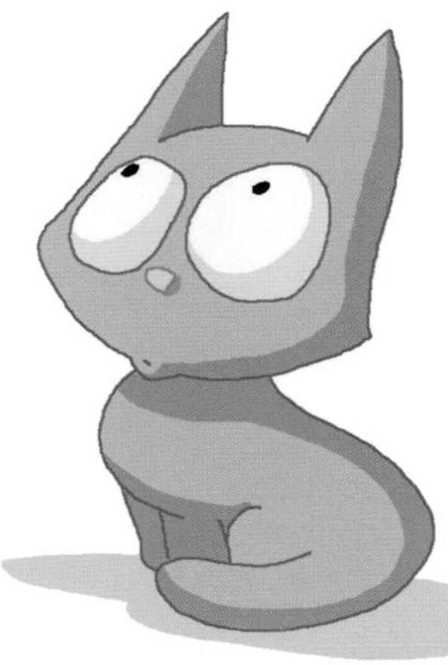

JULIEN NEEL

GRAPHIC UNIVERSE™ · MINNEAPOLIS · NEW YORK

TO MATHILDE
TO MAMIE AND MONSIEUR PAPA

Story and art by Julien Neel

Translation by Carol Klio Burrell

First American edition published in 2012 by Graphic Universe™.

Lou! by Julien Neel © 2006 — Glénat Editions
© 2012 Lerner Publishing Group, Inc., for the U.S. edition

Graphic Universe™ is a trademark of Lerner Publishing Group, Inc.

Graphic Universe™
A division of Lerner Publishing Group, Inc.
241 First Avenue North
Minneapolis, MN 55401 U.S.A.

Website address: www.lernerbooks.com

Library of Congress Cataloging-in-Publication Data

Neel, Julien.
   [Cimetière des autobus. English]
   Down in the dumps / written and illustrated by Julien Neel ; translation by Carol
Klio Burrell. — 1st American ed.
      p.   cm. — (Lou! ; #3)
   Summary: Lou finds it confusing and difficult to be thirteen, especially with her
mother and Richard's romance heating up, being separated from her best friend
Mina at school, and getting another letter from Paul when she never answered the
first one.
   ISBN 978–0–7613–8779–4 (lib. bdg. : alk. paper)
   [1. Graphic novels 2. Mothers and daughters—Fiction. 3. Best friends—Fiction.
4. Friendship—Fiction. 5. Junior high schools—Fiction. 6. Schools—Fiction.
7. Dating (Social customs)—Fiction. 8. Graphic novels] I. Burrell, Carol Klio. II. Title.
PZ7.7.N44Dow 2012
741.5'944—dc23   2012003973

Manufactured in the United States of America
1 – DP – 7/15/12

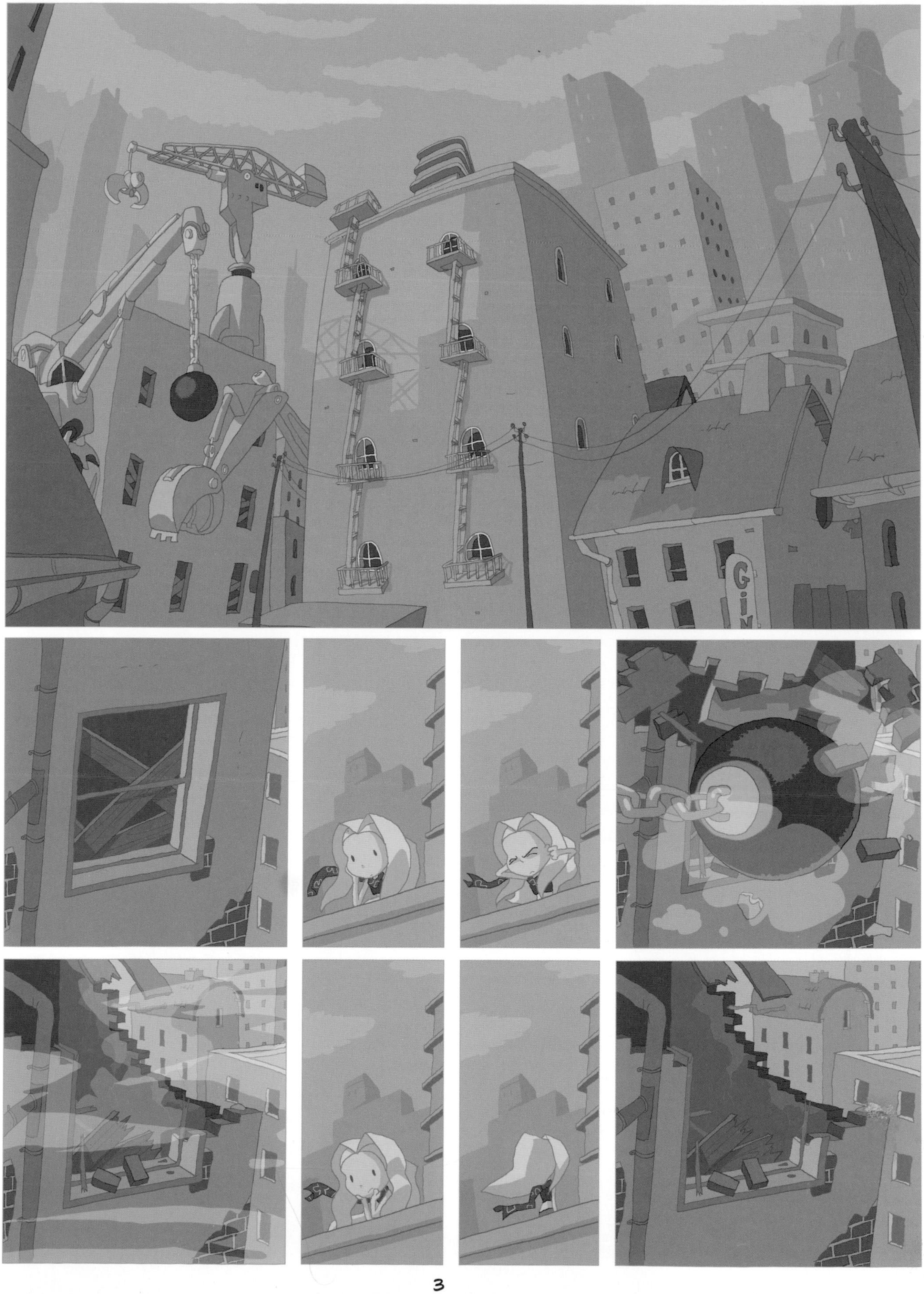

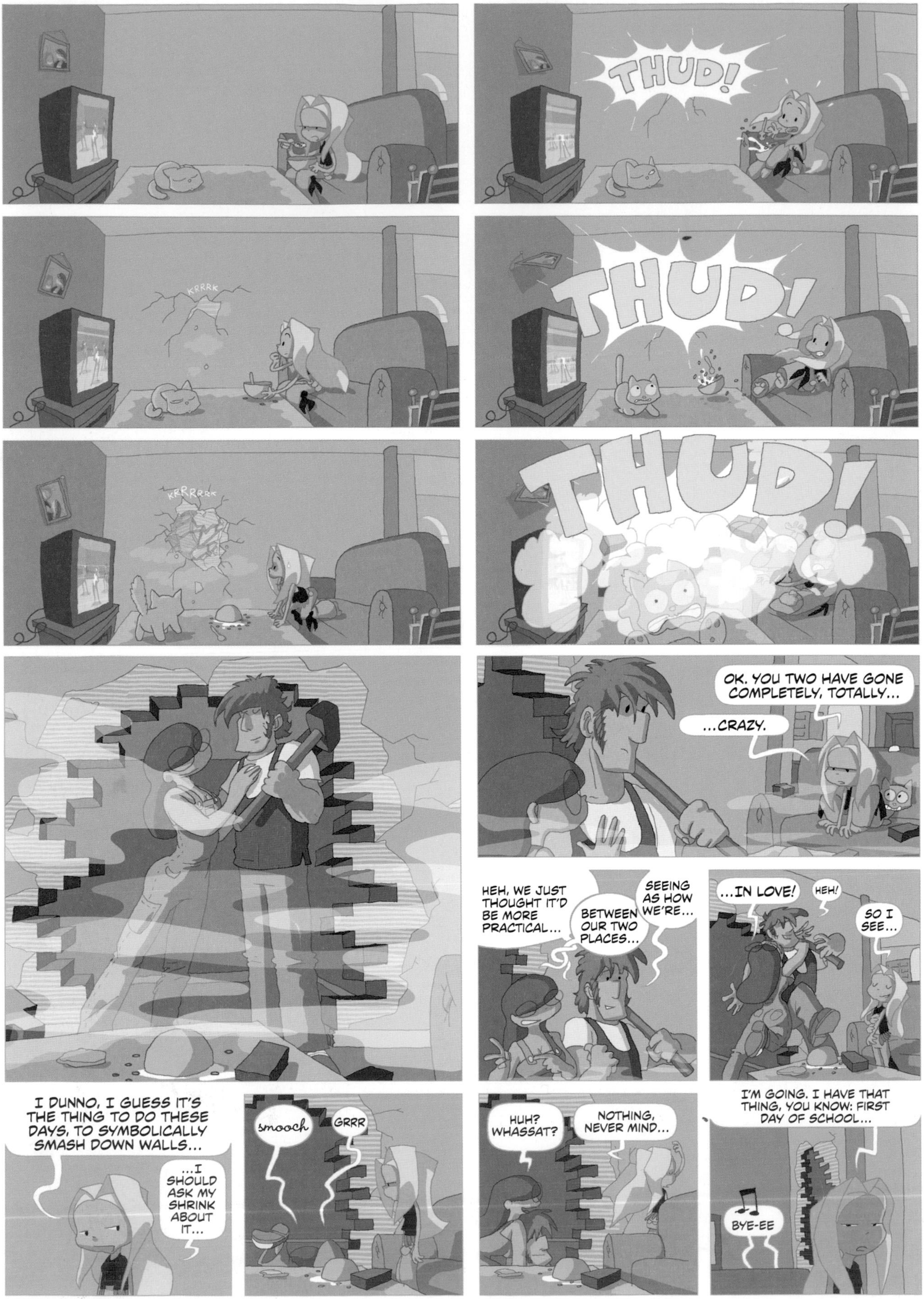
THUD!
KRRRK
THUD!
KRRRRRK
THUD!
OK. YOU TWO HAVE GONE COMPLETELY, TOTALLY...
...CRAZY.
HEH, WE JUST THOUGHT IT'D BE MORE PRACTICAL...
BETWEEN OUR TWO PLACES...
SEEING AS HOW WE'RE...
...IN LOVE!
HEH!
SO I SEE...
I DUNNO, I GUESS IT'S THE THING TO DO THESE DAYS, TO SYMBOLICALLY SMASH DOWN WALLS...
...I SHOULD ASK MY SHRINK ABOUT IT...
smooch
GRRR
HUH? WHASSAT?
NOTHING, NEVER MIND...
I'M GOING. I HAVE THAT THING, YOU KNOW: FIRST DAY OF SCHOOL...
BYE-EE

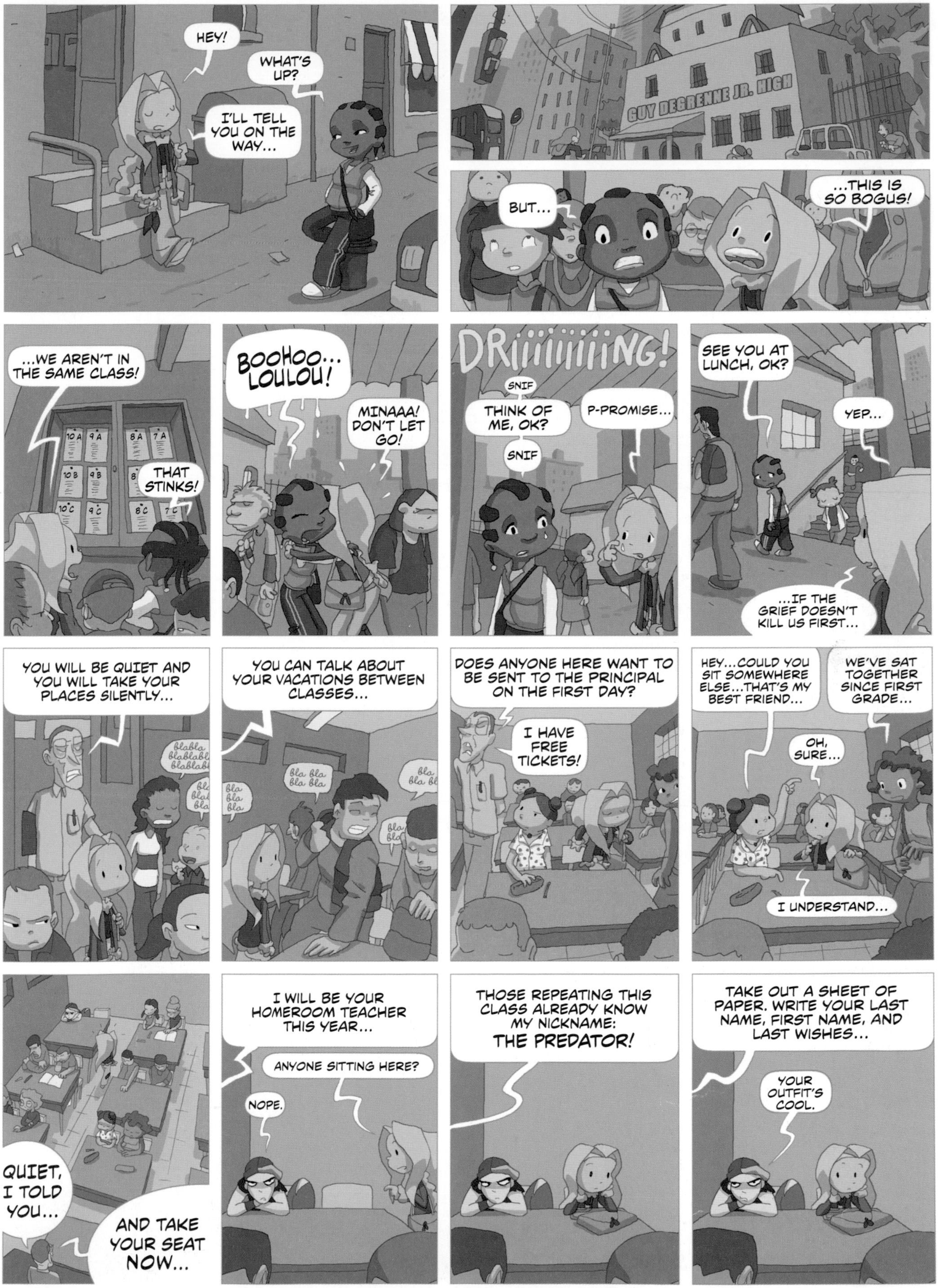
HEY!
WHAT'S UP?
I'LL TELL YOU ON THE WAY...
GUY DEGRENNE JR. HIGH
BUT...
...THIS IS SO BOGUS!
...WE AREN'T IN THE SAME CLASS!
THAT STINKS!
BOOHOO... LOULOU!
MINAAA! DON'T LET GO!
DRiiiiiiiiiNG!
SNIF
THINK OF ME, OK?
SNIF
P-PROMISE...
SEE YOU AT LUNCH, OK?
YEP...
...IF THE GRIEF DOESN'T KILL US FIRST...
YOU WILL BE QUIET AND YOU WILL TAKE YOUR PLACES SILENTLY...
YOU CAN TALK ABOUT YOUR VACATIONS BETWEEN CLASSES...
DOES ANYONE HERE WANT TO BE SENT TO THE PRINCIPAL ON THE FIRST DAY?
I HAVE FREE TICKETS!
HEY...COULD YOU SIT SOMEWHERE ELSE...THAT'S MY BEST FRIEND...
WE'VE SAT TOGETHER SINCE FIRST GRADE...
OH, SURE...
I UNDERSTAND...
QUIET, I TOLD YOU...
AND TAKE YOUR SEAT NOW...
I WILL BE YOUR HOMEROOM TEACHER THIS YEAR...
ANYONE SITTING HERE?
NOPE.
THOSE REPEATING THIS CLASS ALREADY KNOW MY NICKNAME: THE PREDATOR!
TAKE OUT A SHEET OF PAPER. WRITE YOUR LAST NAME, FIRST NAME, AND LAST WISHES...
YOUR OUTFIT'S COOL.

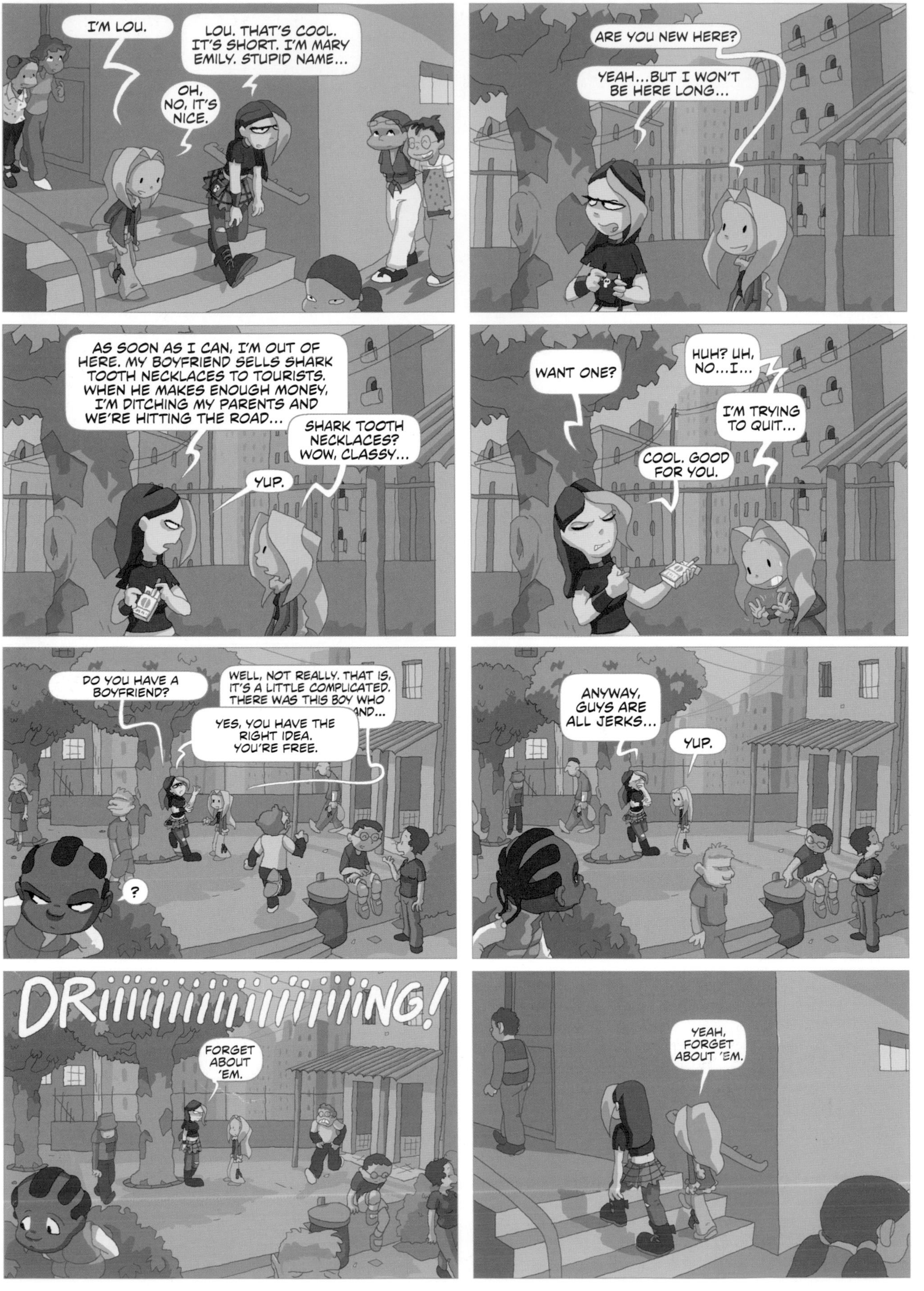
I'M LOU.
LOU. THAT'S COOL. IT'S SHORT. I'M MARY EMILY. STUPID NAME...
OH, NO, IT'S NICE.
ARE YOU NEW HERE?
YEAH...BUT I WON'T BE HERE LONG...
AS SOON AS I CAN, I'M OUT OF HERE. MY BOYFRIEND SELLS SHARK TOOTH NECKLACES TO TOURISTS. WHEN HE MAKES ENOUGH MONEY, I'M DITCHING MY PARENTS AND WE'RE HITTING THE ROAD...
SHARK TOOTH NECKLACES? WOW, CLASSY...
YUP.
WANT ONE?
HUH? UH, NO...I...
I'M TRYING TO QUIT...
COOL. GOOD FOR YOU.
DO YOU HAVE A BOYFRIEND?
WELL, NOT REALLY. THAT IS, IT'S A LITTLE COMPLICATED. THERE WAS THIS BOY WHO
AND...
YES, YOU HAVE THE RIGHT IDEA. YOU'RE FREE.
?
ANYWAY, GUYS ARE ALL JERKS...
YUP.
DRiiiiiiiiiiiiiiiiiiiNG!
FORGET ABOUT 'EM.
YEAH, FORGET ABOUT 'EM.

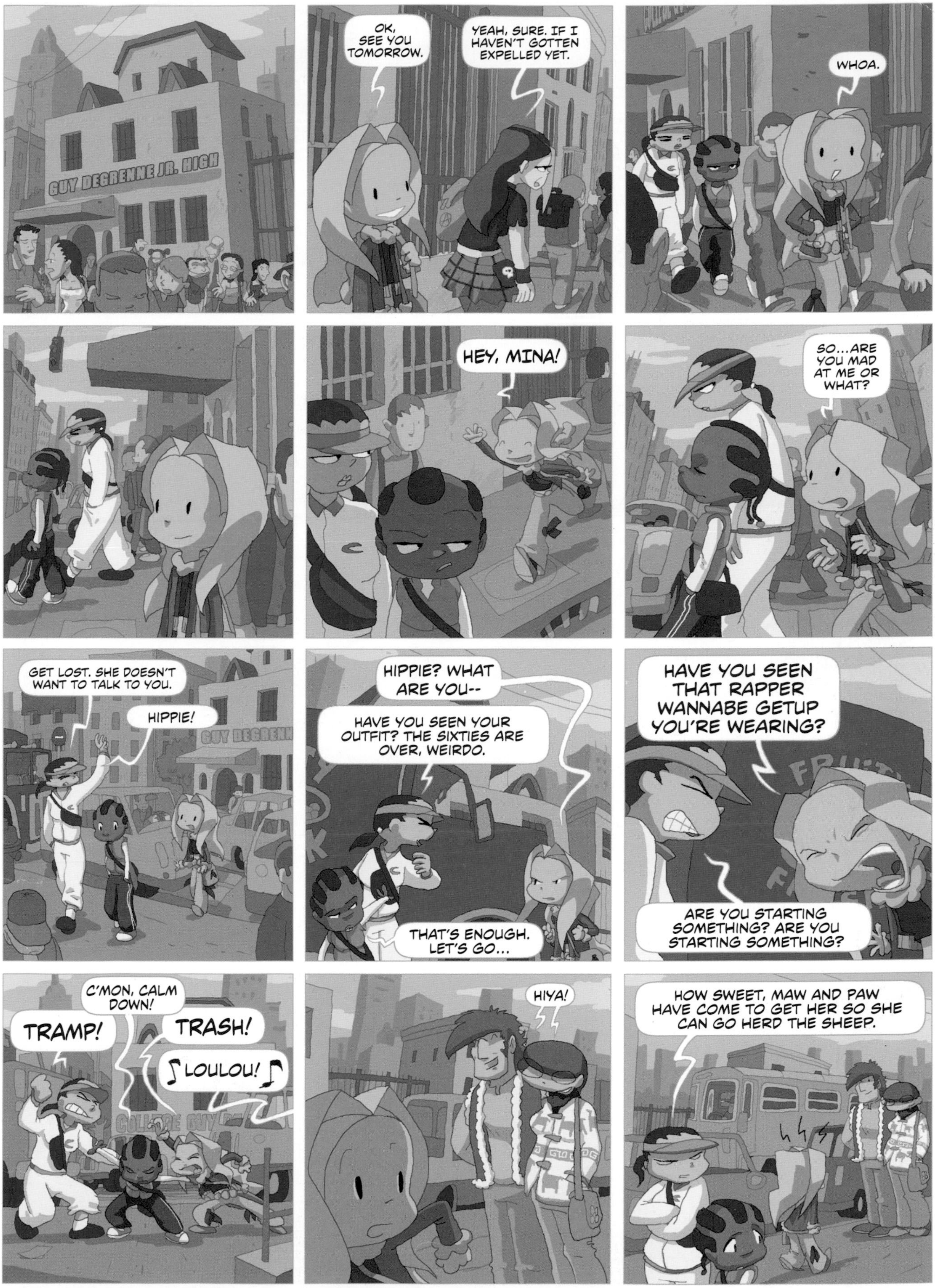
GUY DEGRENNE JR. HIGH
OK, SEE YOU TOMORROW.
YEAH, SURE. IF I HAVEN'T GOTTEN EXPELLED YET.
WHOA.
HEY, MINA!
SO...ARE YOU MAD AT ME OR WHAT?
GET LOST. SHE DOESN'T WANT TO TALK TO YOU.
HIPPIE!
HIPPIE? WHAT ARE YOU--
HAVE YOU SEEN YOUR OUTFIT? THE SIXTIES ARE OVER, WEIRDO.
THAT'S ENOUGH. LET'S GO...
HAVE YOU SEEN THAT RAPPER WANNABE GETUP YOU'RE WEARING?
ARE YOU STARTING SOMETHING? ARE YOU STARTING SOMETHING?
C'MON, CALM DOWN!
TRAMP!
TRASH!
LOULOU!
HIYA!
HOW SWEET, MAW AND PAW HAVE COME TO GET HER SO SHE CAN GO HERD THE SHEEP.

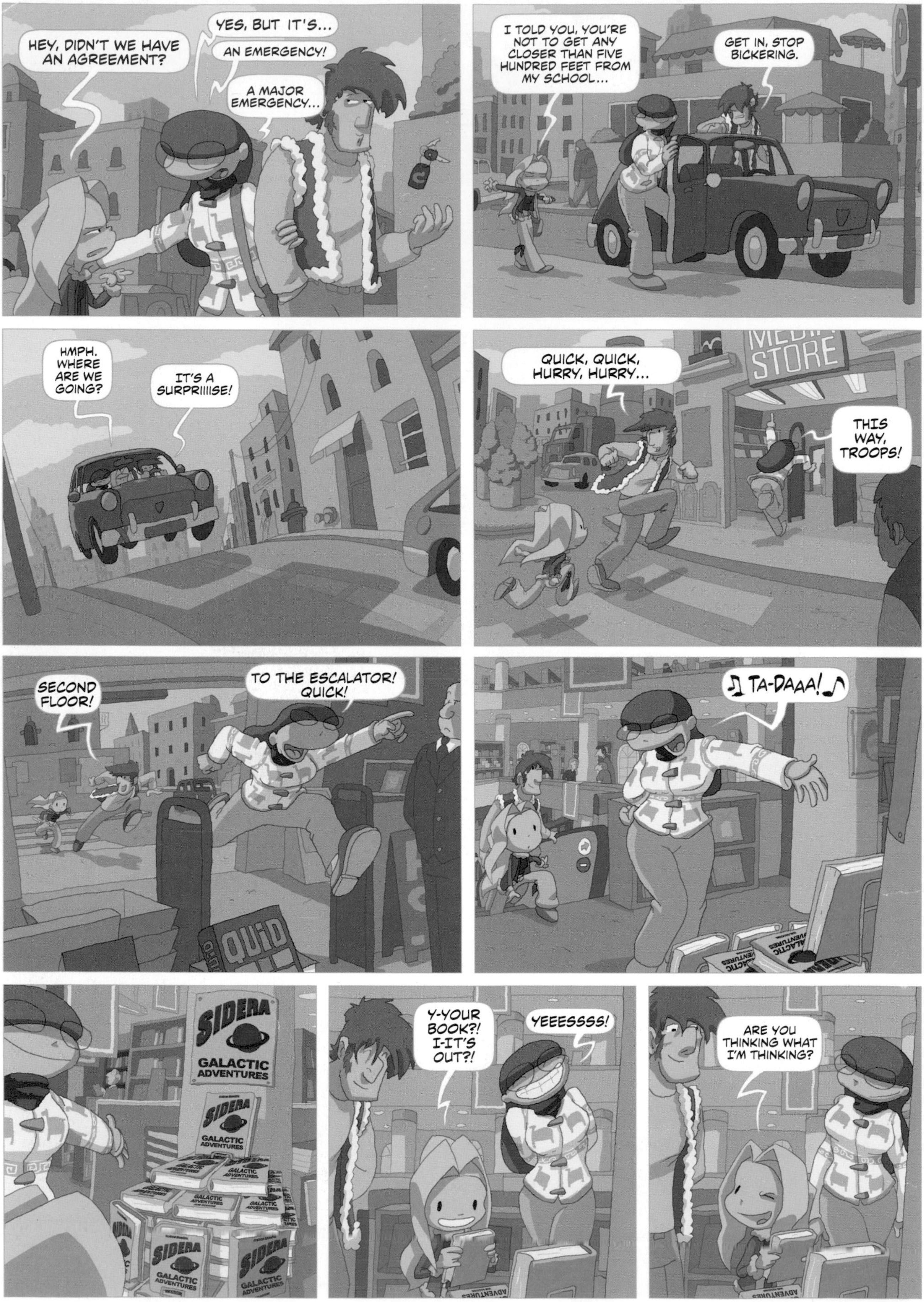
HEY, DIDN'T WE HAVE AN AGREEMENT?
YES, BUT IT'S...
AN EMERGENCY!
A MAJOR EMERGENCY...
I TOLD YOU, YOU'RE NOT TO GET ANY CLOSER THAN FIVE HUNDRED FEET FROM MY SCHOOL...
GET IN, STOP BICKERING.
HMPH. WHERE ARE WE GOING?
IT'S A SURPRIIIISE!
MEDIA STORE
QUICK, QUICK, HURRY, HURRY...
THIS WAY, TROOPS!
SECOND FLOOR!
TO THE ESCALATOR! QUICK!
♫ TA-DAAA! ♪
SIDERA
GALACTIC ADVENTURES
Y-YOUR BOOK?! I-IT'S OUT?!
YEEESSSS!
ARE YOU THINKING WHAT I'M THINKING?

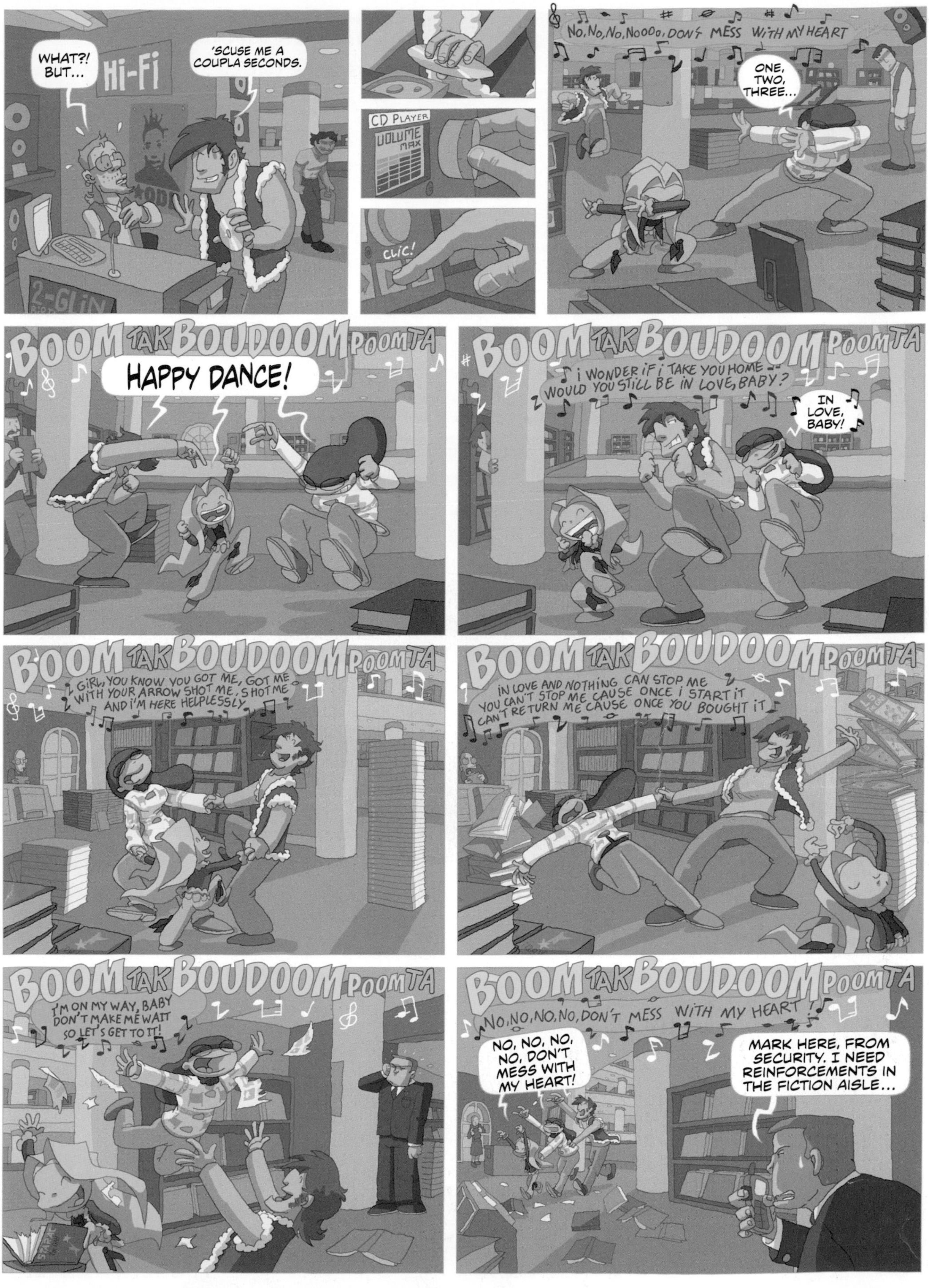
WHAT?! BUT...
'SCUSE ME A COUPLA SECONDS.
Hi-Fi
2-GLIN
CD PLAYER
VOLUME MAX
CLIC!
No, No, No, Noooo, DON'T MESS WITH MY HEART
ONE, TWO, THREE...
BOOM TAK BOUDOOM POOMTA
HAPPY DANCE!
BOOM TAK BOUDOOM POOMTA
I WONDER IF I TAKE YOU HOME WOULD YOU STILL BE IN LOVE, BABY?
IN LOVE, BABY!
BOOM TAK BOUDOOM POOMTA
GIRL, YOU KNOW YOU GOT ME, GOT ME WITH YOUR ARROW SHOT ME, SHOT ME AND I'M HERE HELPLESSLY
BOOM TAK BOUDOOM POOMTA
IN LOVE AND NOTHING CAN STOP ME YOU CAN'T STOP ME CAUSE ONCE I START IT CAN'T RETURN ME CAUSE ONCE YOU BOUGHT IT
BOOM TAK BOUDOOM POOMTA
I'M ON MY WAY, BABY DON'T MAKE ME WAIT SO LET'S GET TO IT!
BOOM TAK BOUDOOM POOMTA
NO, NO, NO, NO, DON'T MESS WITH MY HEART!
NO, NO, NO, NO, DON'T MESS WITH MY HEART!
MARK HERE, FROM SECURITY. I NEED REINFORCEMENTS IN THE FICTION AISLE...

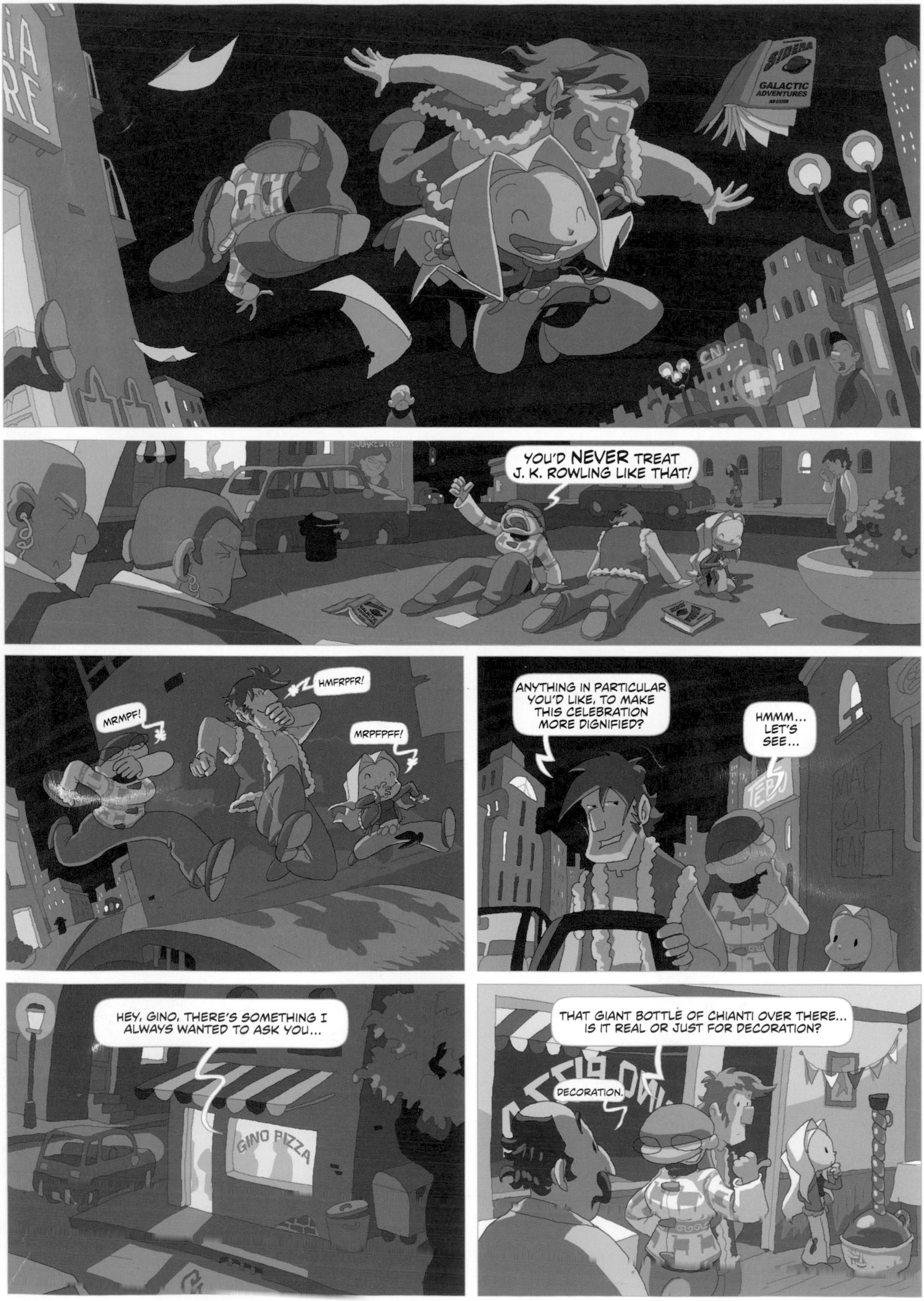
GALACTIC ADVENTURES
YOU'D **NEVER** TREAT J. K. ROWLING LIKE THAT!
MRMPF!
HMFRPFR!
MRPFPFF!
ANYTHING IN PARTICULAR YOU'D LIKE, TO MAKE THIS CELEBRATION MORE DIGNIFIED?
HMMM... LET'S SEE...
HEY, GINO, THERE'S SOMETHING I ALWAYS WANTED TO ASK YOU...
GINO PIZZA
THAT GIANT BOTTLE OF CHIANTI OVER THERE... IS IT REAL OR JUST FOR DECORATION?
DECORATION.

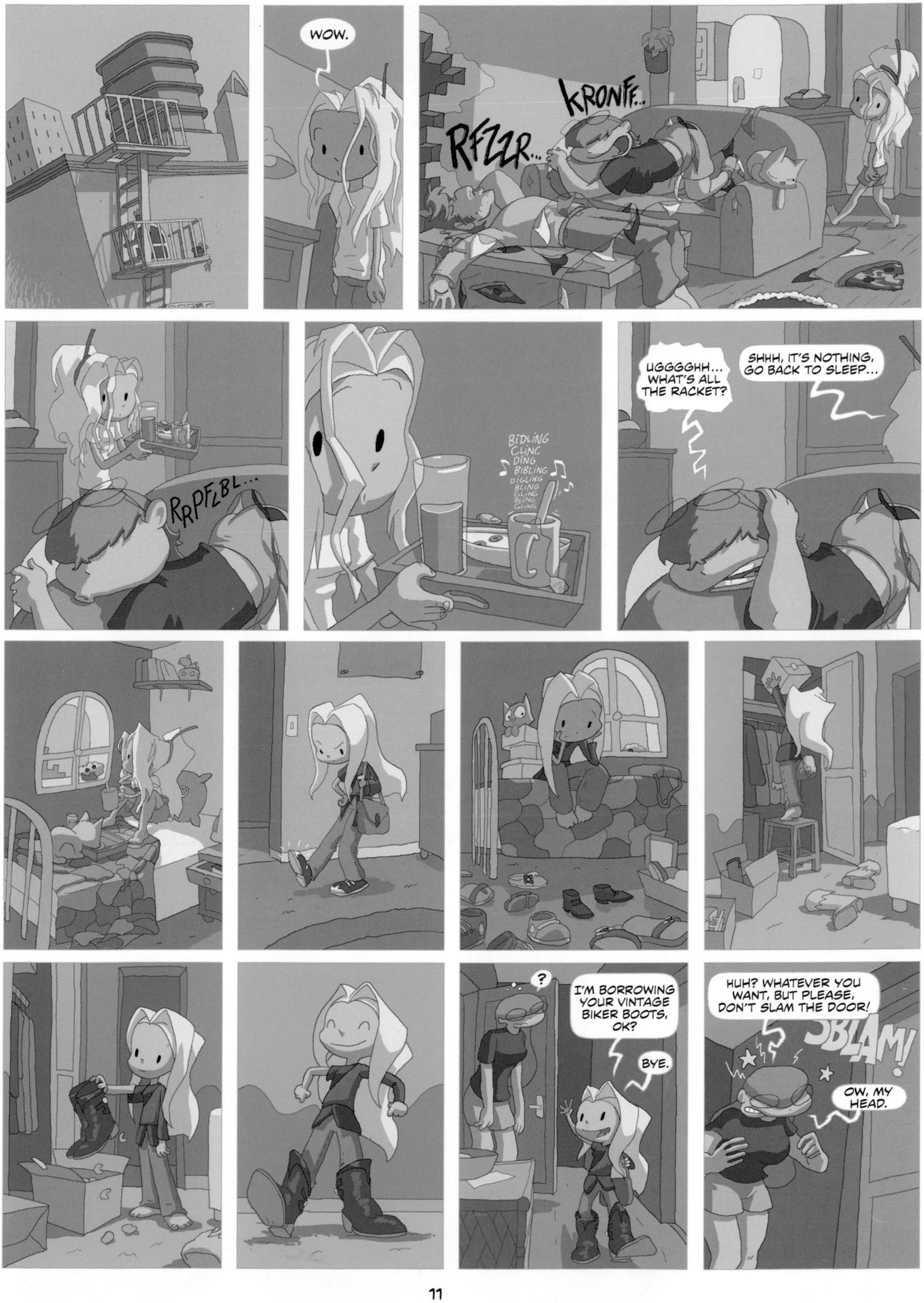
WOW.
KRONFF...
RFZZR...
RRPFLBL...
BIDLING
CLINC
DING
BIBLING
DIGLING
BLING
GLING
BLING
GLING
UGGGGHH... WHAT'S ALL THE RACKET?
SHHH, IT'S NOTHING, GO BACK TO SLEEP...
?
I'M BORROWING YOUR VINTAGE BIKER BOOTS, OK?
BYE.
HUH? WHATEVER YOU WANT, BUT PLEASE, DON'T SLAM THE DOOR!
SBLAM!
OW, MY HEAD.

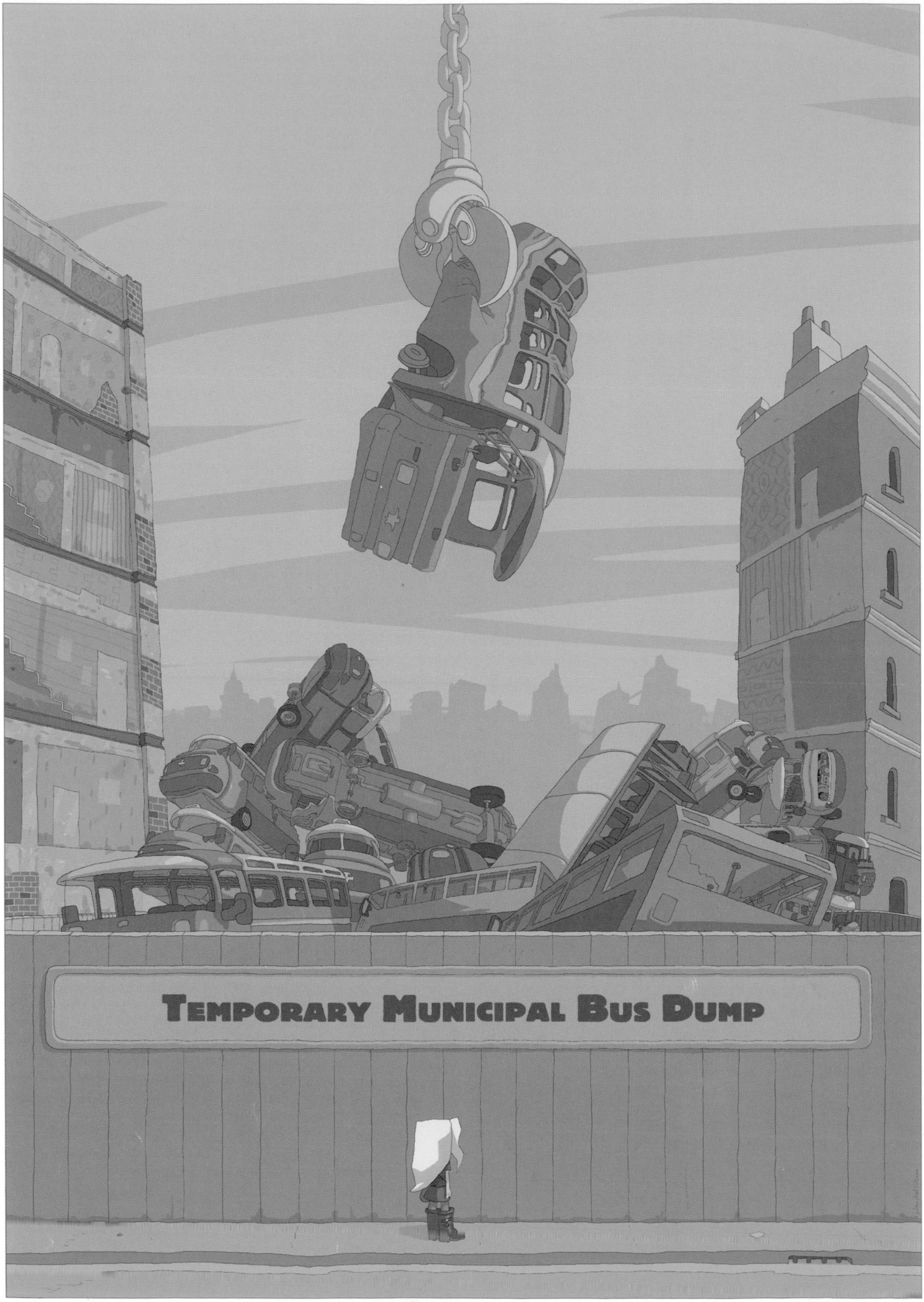
TEMPORARY MUNICIPAL BUS DUMP

A BUS CEMETERY.

RIGHT ACROSS FROM ME.

WHERE TRISTAN WAS...

ALL TORN DOWN.

THE BUILDING, NOT TRISTAN.

TRISTAN, YOU KNOW, THE BOY WHO...

...WHO MOVED TO ANOTHER CITY.

AND WHO I REALLY LIKED AND THEN ZIP...

NOT A PEEP.

I DON'T KNOW WHY.

I...

ANYWAY...

THERE'S THIS OTHER BOY.

PAUL.

WHO I MET AT MEMAW'S...

BUT WE DON'T LIKE EACH OTHER THAT WAY.

I DON'T THINK SO, ANYWAY...

IT'S JUST THAT HE WASN'T...UM...

HE WAS TOO...

OR IT WAS SUMMER VACATION THAT MADE US...UH...

TRISTAN AND ME, I MEAN.

ANYWAY, YOU SEE, THAT IS--NO: FOR EXAMPLE, MY MOTHER...

AND RICHARD...

OUR NEIGHBOR.

THE OTHER ONE.

THERE THEY ARE.

BOOM.

IN LOVE!

...AND THAT AWFUL CLEMENT FIFFER.

HEHE!

SO, THEY KNOCKED DOWN THE WALL BETWEEN OUR APARTMENTS.

THAT WAS A SHOCK.

THEN THE FIRST DAY OF SCHOOL.

BLAH! AND THEN AT SCHOOL, BLAH BLAH BLAH...

I HAD A HUGE FIGHT WITH MINA.

I DON'T EVEN KNOW IF WE'RE STILL FRIENDS...

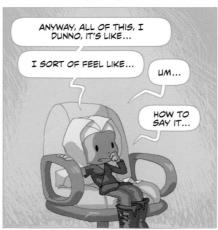

ANYWAY, ALL OF THIS, I DUNNO, IT'S LIKE...

I SORT OF FEEL LIKE...

UM...

HOW TO SAY IT...

CONFUSED?

THAT'S IT!

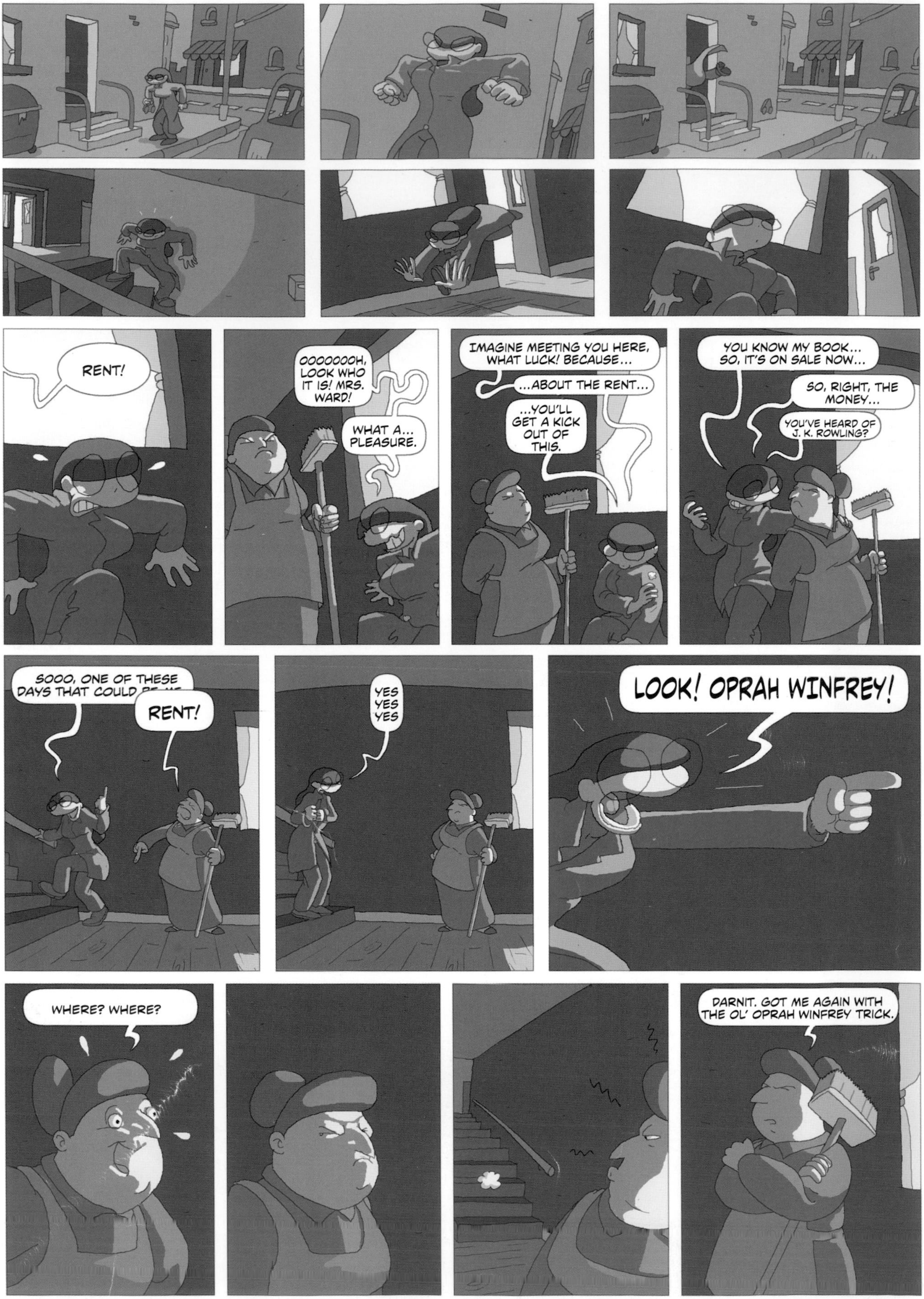
RENT!
OOOOOOOH, LOOK WHO IT IS! MRS. WARD!
WHAT A... PLEASURE.
IMAGINE MEETING YOU HERE, WHAT LUCK! BECAUSE...
...ABOUT THE RENT...
...YOU'LL GET A KICK OUT OF THIS.
YOU KNOW MY BOOK... SO, IT'S ON SALE NOW...
SO, RIGHT, THE MONEY...
YOU'VE HEARD OF J. K. ROWLING?
SOOO, ONE OF THESE DAYS THAT COULD
RENT!
YES YES YES
LOOK! OPRAH WINFREY!
WHERE? WHERE?
DARNIT. GOT ME AGAIN WITH THE OL' OPRAH WINFREY TRICK.

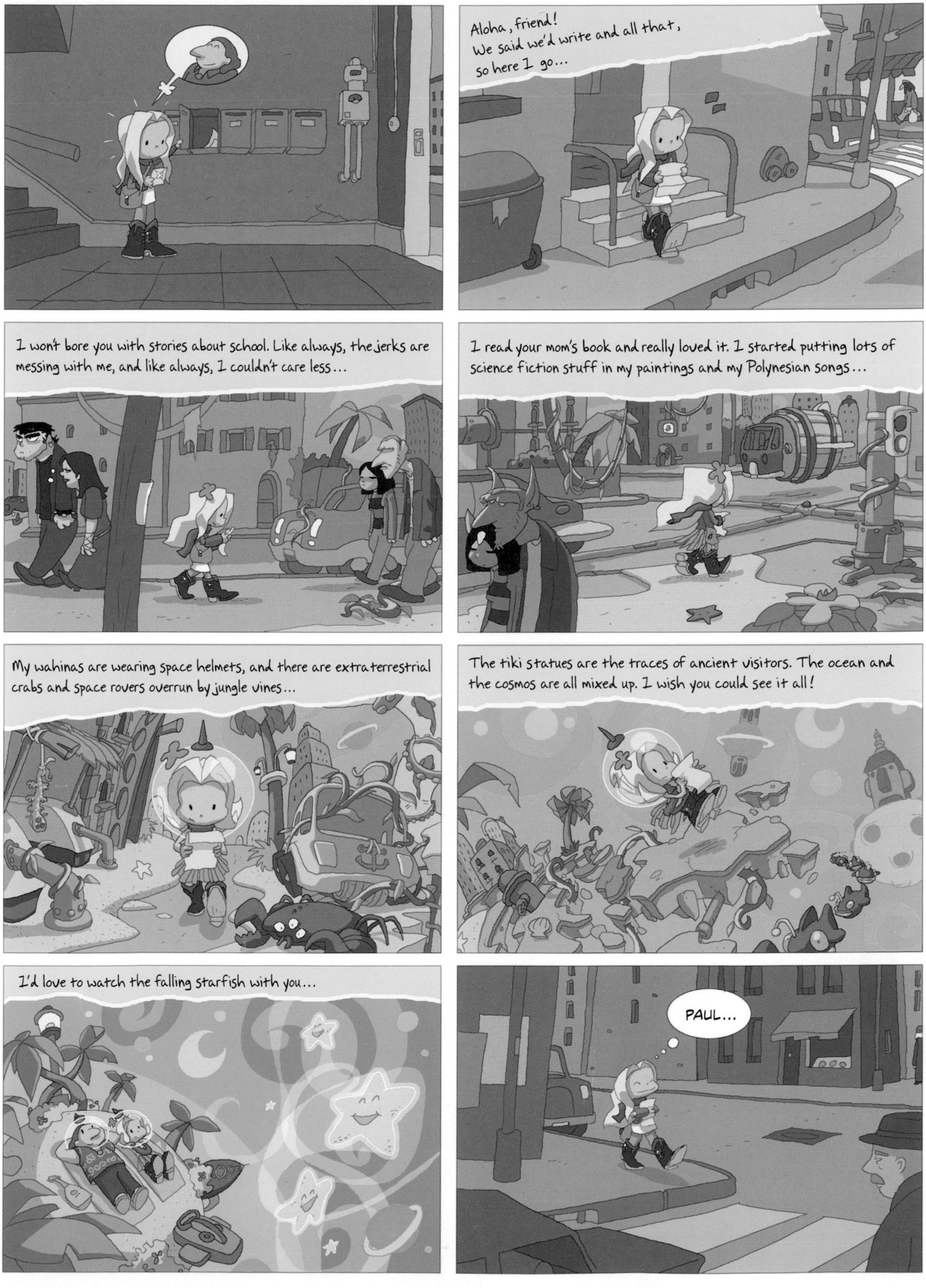
Aloha, friend!
We said we'd write and all that,
so here I go...
I won't bore you with stories about school. Like always, the jerks are messing with me, and like always, I couldn't care less...
I read your mom's book and really loved it. I started putting lots of science fiction stuff in my paintings and my Polynesian songs...
My wahinas are wearing space helmets, and there are extraterrestrial crabs and space rovers overrun by jungle vines...
The tiki statues are the traces of ancient visitors. The ocean and the cosmos are all mixed up. I wish you could see it all!
I'd love to watch the falling starfish with you...
PAUL...

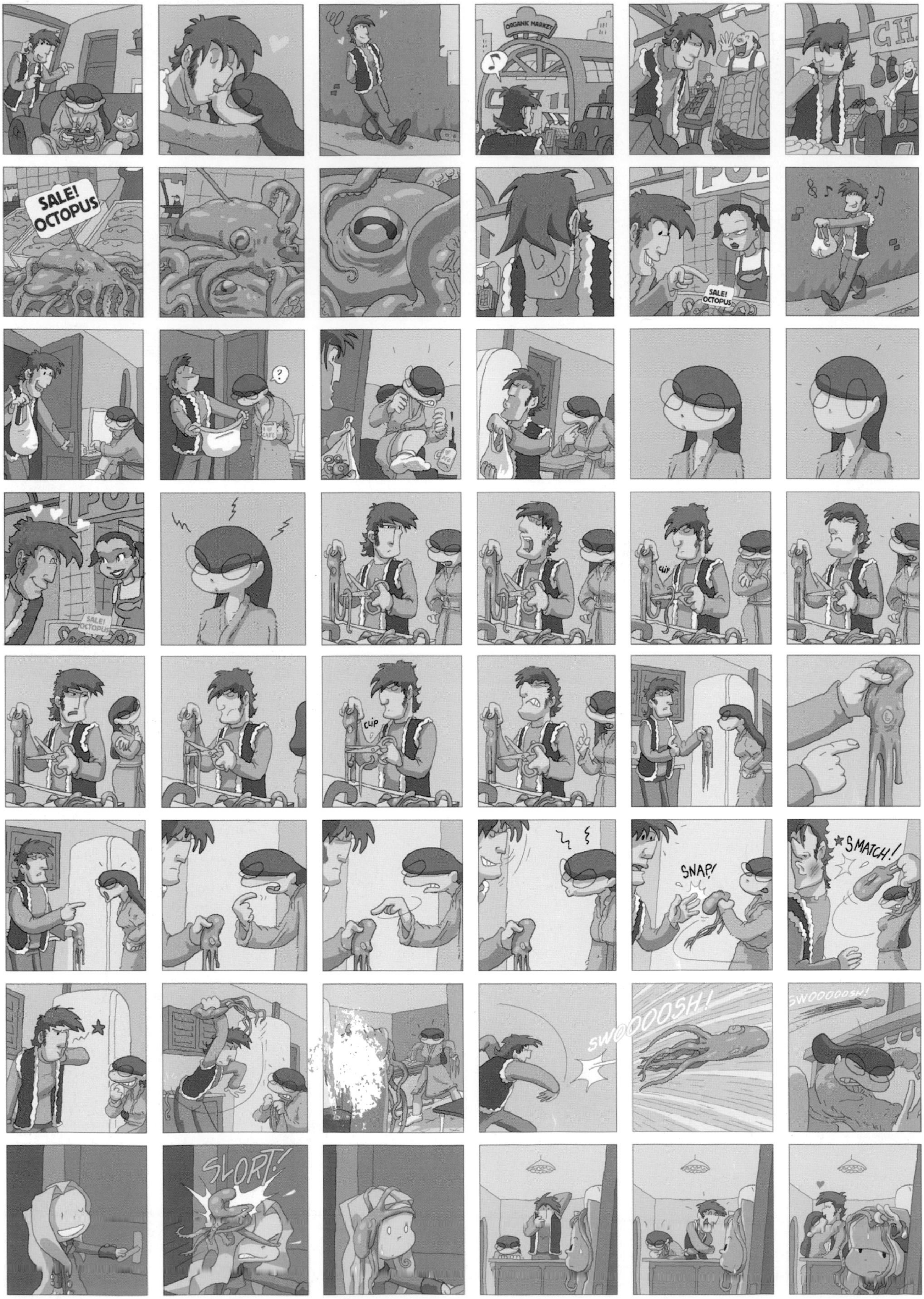
ORGANIC MARKET
SALE! OCTOPUS
SALE! OCTOPUS
SALE! OCTOPUS
clip
clip
SNAP!
SMATCH!
SWOOOOSH!
SWOOOOOSH!
SLORT!

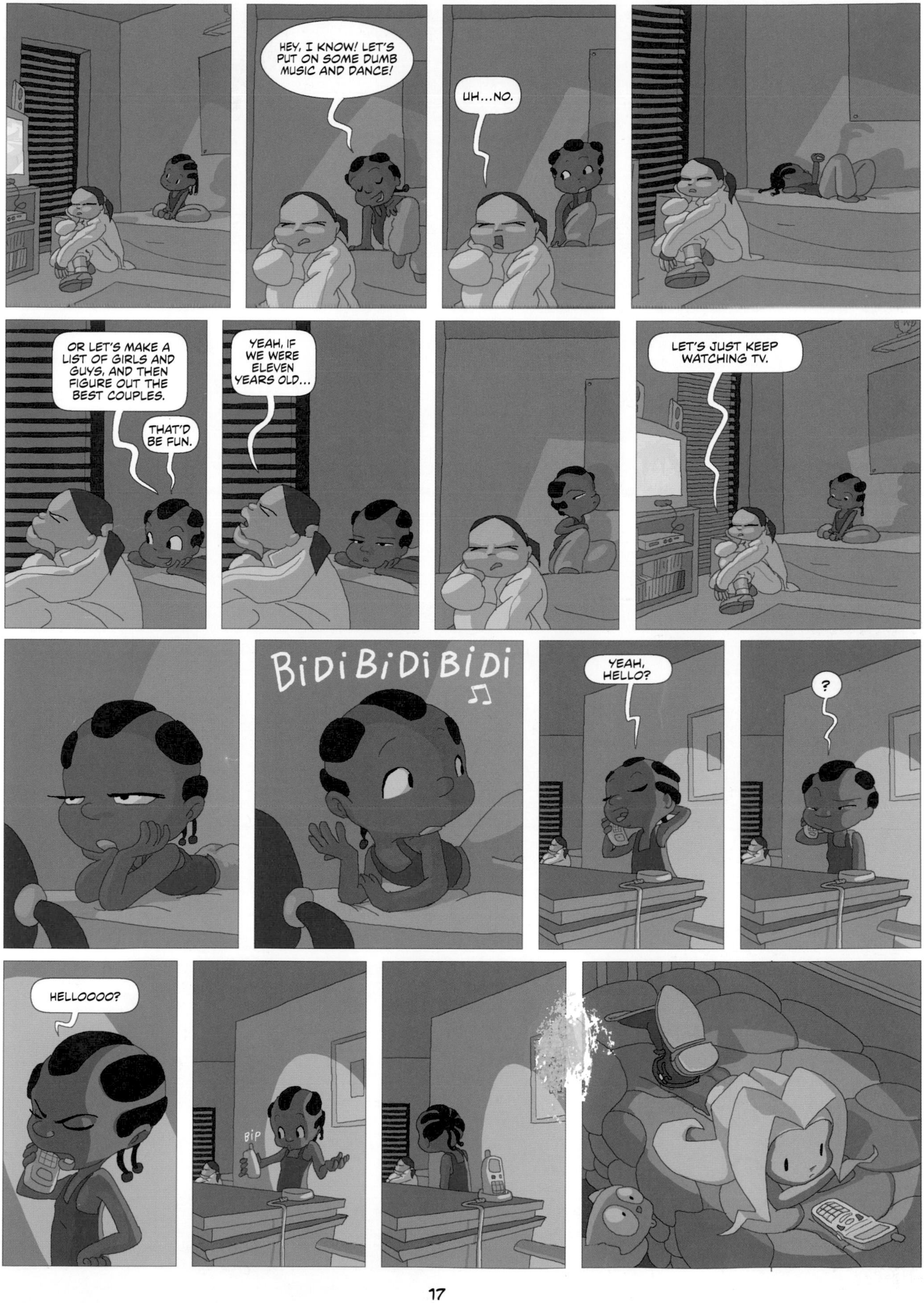
HEY, I KNOW! LET'S PUT ON SOME DUMB MUSIC AND DANCE!
UH...NO.
OR LET'S MAKE A LIST OF GIRLS AND GUYS, AND THEN FIGURE OUT THE BEST COUPLES.
THAT'D BE FUN.
YEAH, IF WE WERE ELEVEN YEARS OLD...
LET'S JUST KEEP WATCHING TV.
BiDiBiDiBiDi
YEAH, HELLO?
?
HELLOOOO?
BIP

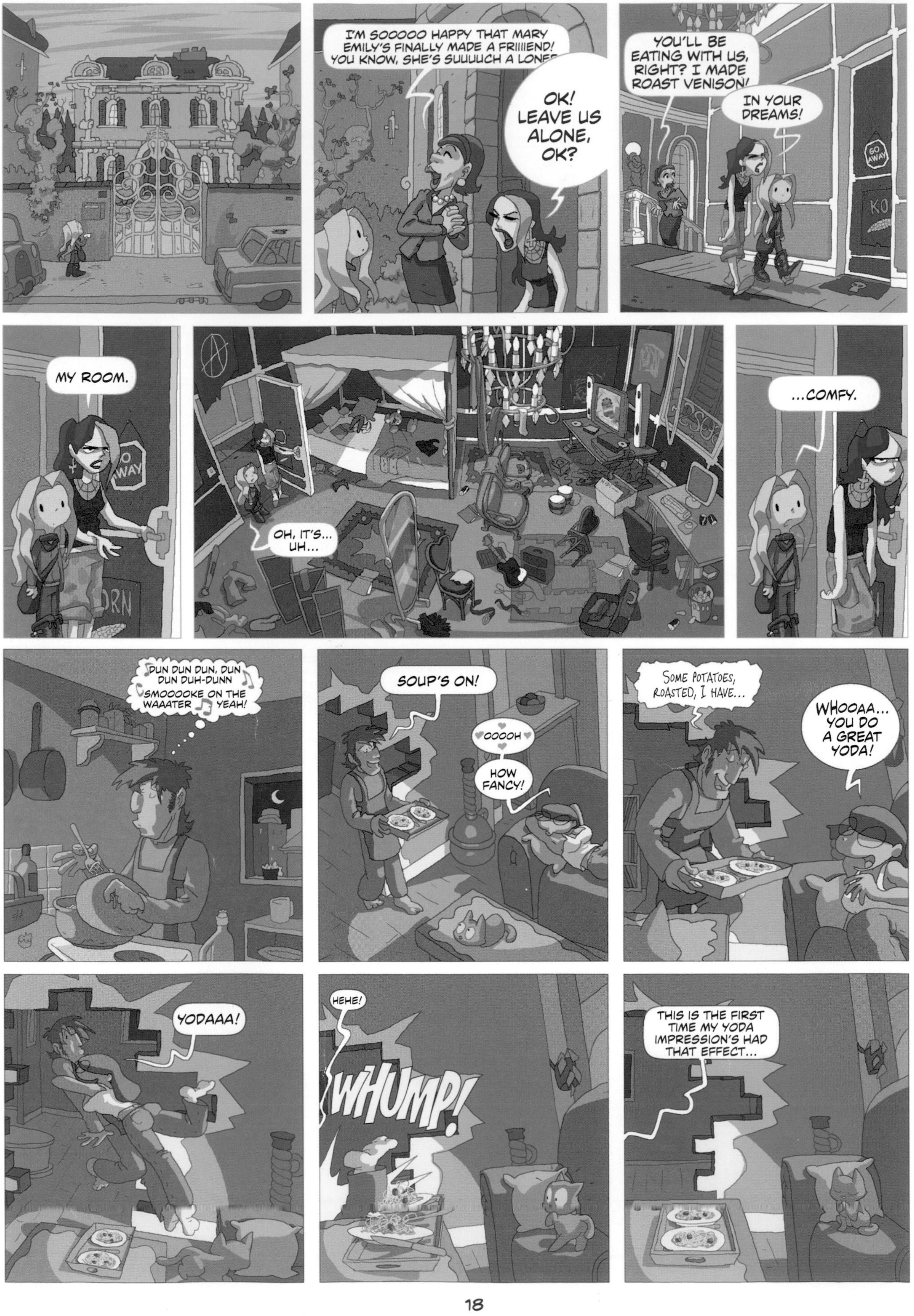
I'M SOOOOO HAPPY THAT MARY EMILY'S FINALLY MADE A FRIIIIEND! YOU KNOW, SHE'S SUUUUCH A LONER
OK! LEAVE US ALONE, OK?
YOU'LL BE EATING WITH US, RIGHT? I MADE ROAST VENISON!
IN YOUR DREAMS!
GO AWAY
MY ROOM.
OH, IT'S... UH...
...COMFY.
DUN DUN DUN, DUN DUN DUH-DUNN SMOOOOKE ON THE WAAATER YEAH!
SOUP'S ON!
OOOOH
HOW FANCY!
SOME POTATOES, ROASTED, I HAVE...
WHOOAA... YOU DO A GREAT YODA!
YODAAA!
HEHE!
WHUMP!
THIS IS THE FIRST TIME MY YODA IMPRESSION'S HAD THAT EFFECT...

...AND THEN THERE'S THIS BOY, PAUL, WHO I MET AT MY GRANDMOTHER'S, IN THE COUNTRY. SURE, HE'S A LITTLE OLDER THAN I A...

YOU HUNGRY?

SLAM!

SLAM!

SLAM! SLAM!

UH...WON'T THAT WAKE YOUR PARENTS?

MY PARENTS CAN GET LOST!

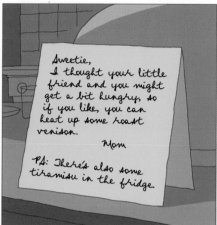

Sweetie,
I thought your little friend and you might get a bit hungry, so if you like, you can heat up some roast venison.
Mom

P.S: There's also some tiramisu in the fridge.

YAY, ROAST VENISON.

GROSS.

CRITCH CRITCH

THE POWER OF THE DARK SIDE UNDERESTIMATE YOU MUST NOT.

HEHE HEHE!

WHERE ARE YOU GOING?

TO CHECK IF THEY'RE TALKING ABOUT MY BOOK ON THE INTERNET!

SLURP.

AW, TOO BAD, IT'S GOTTEN COLD NOW.

HEY! DARKOVERLORD GAVE SIDERA FOUR OUT OF FIVE LIGHTSABERS ON SCIFIGEEKERY.COM!

FOUR LIGHTSABERS! YEEHAW!

HEHE!

WHUMP!

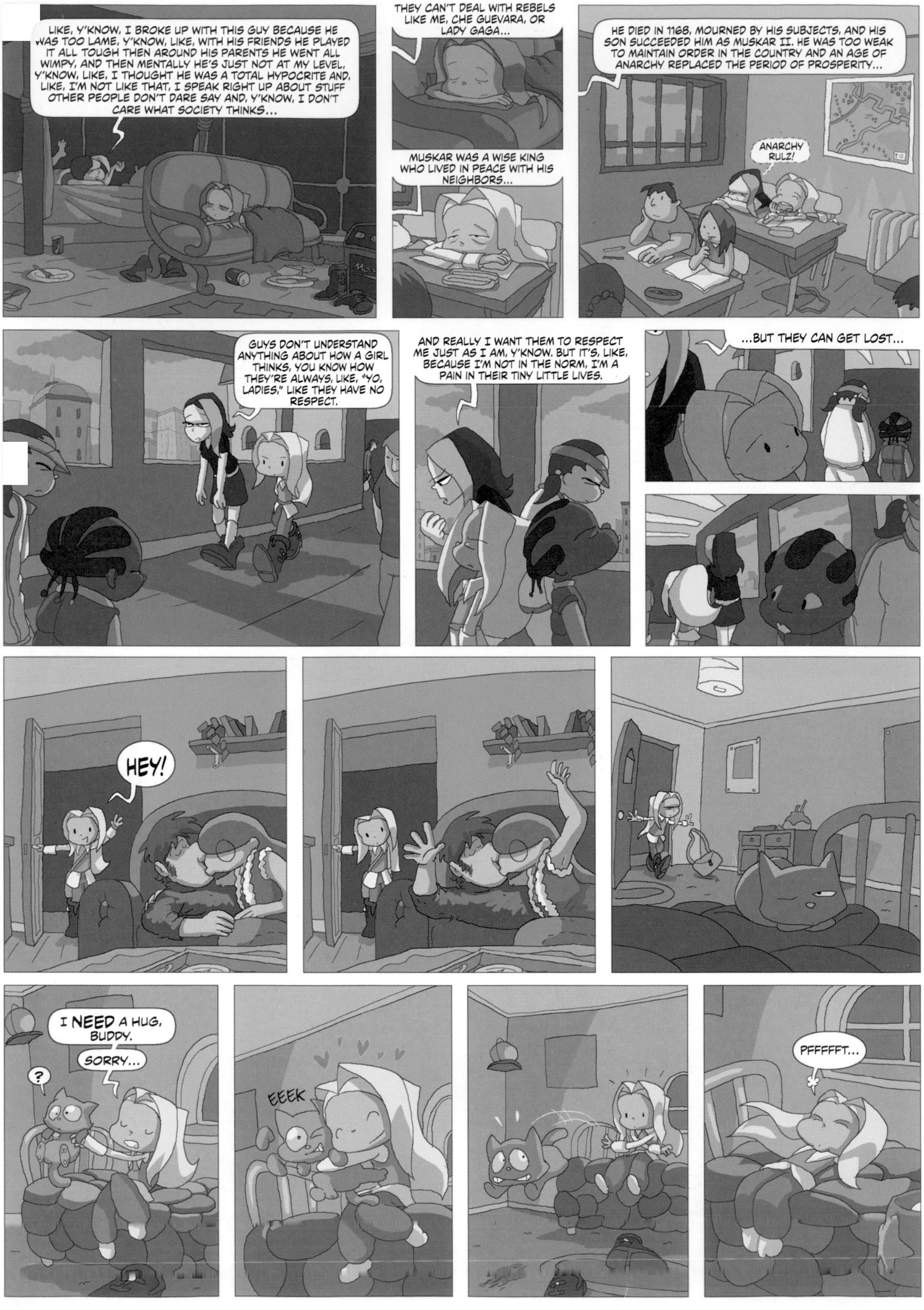
LIKE, Y'KNOW, I BROKE UP WITH THIS GUY BECAUSE HE WAS TOO LAME, Y'KNOW, LIKE, WITH HIS FRIENDS HE PLAYED IT ALL TOUGH THEN AROUND HIS PARENTS HE WENT ALL WIMPY, AND THEN MENTALLY HE'S JUST NOT AT MY LEVEL, Y'KNOW, LIKE, I THOUGHT HE WAS A TOTAL HYPOCRITE AND, LIKE, I'M NOT LIKE THAT, I SPEAK RIGHT UP ABOUT STUFF OTHER PEOPLE DON'T DARE SAY AND, Y'KNOW, I DON'T CARE WHAT SOCIETY THINKS...
THEY CAN'T DEAL WITH REBELS LIKE ME, CHE GUEVARA, OR LADY GAGA...
MUSKAR WAS A WISE KING WHO LIVED IN PEACE WITH HIS NEIGHBORS...
HE DIED IN 1168, MOURNED BY HIS SUBJECTS, AND HIS SON SUCCEEDED HIM AS MUSKAR II. HE WAS TOO WEAK TO MAINTAIN ORDER IN THE COUNTRY AND AN AGE OF ANARCHY REPLACED THE PERIOD OF PROSPERITY...
ANARCHY RULZ!
GUYS DON'T UNDERSTAND ANYTHING ABOUT HOW A GIRL THINKS, YOU KNOW HOW THEY'RE ALWAYS, LIKE, "YO, LADIES," LIKE THEY HAVE NO RESPECT.
AND REALLY I WANT THEM TO RESPECT ME JUST AS I AM, Y'KNOW. BUT IT'S, LIKE, BECAUSE I'M NOT IN THE NORM, I'M A PAIN IN THEIR TINY LITTLE LIVES.
...BUT THEY CAN GET LOST...
HEY!
I NEED A HUG, BUDDY.
SORRY...
?
EEEK
PFFFFFT...

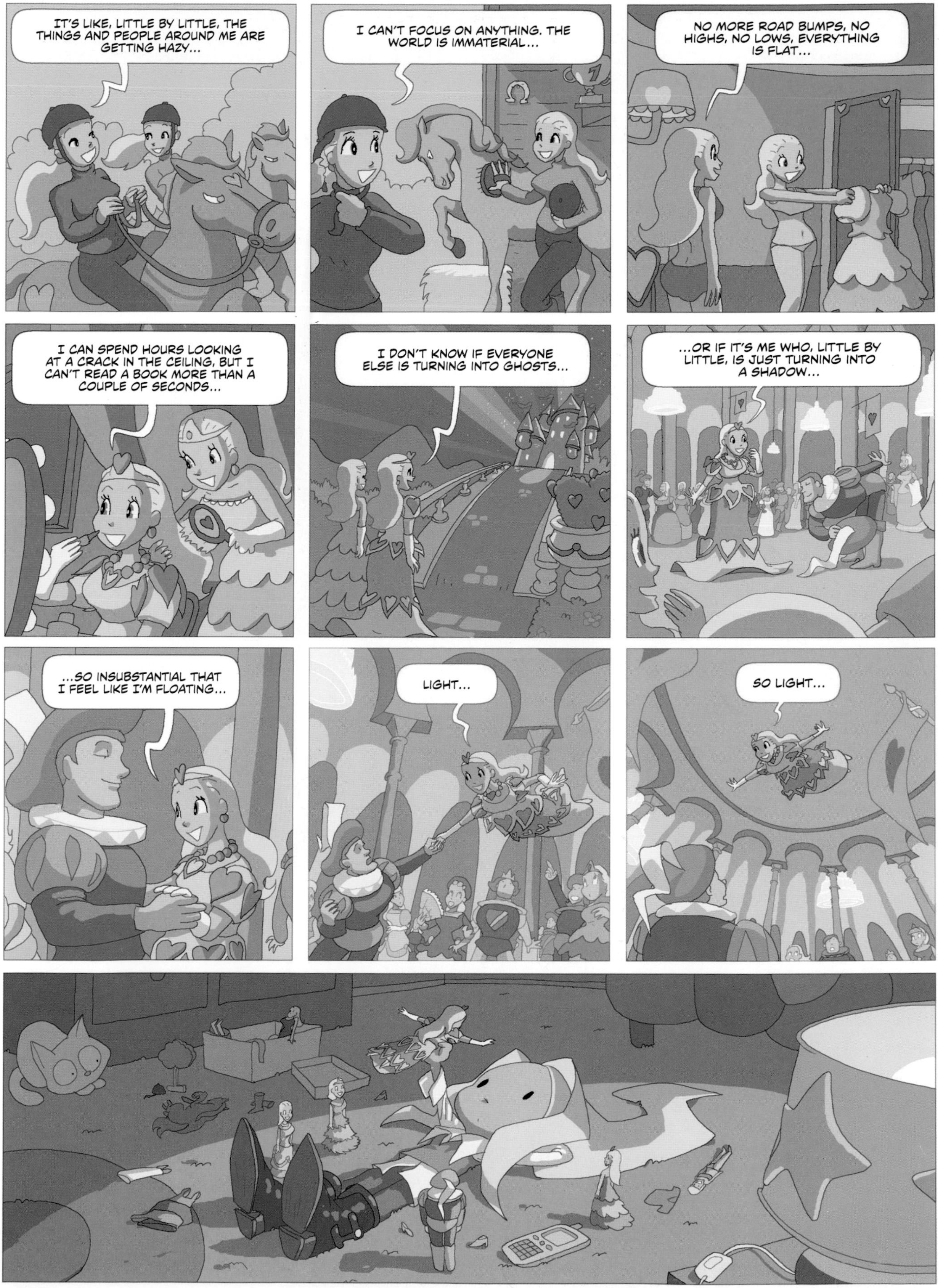
IT'S LIKE, LITTLE BY LITTLE, THE THINGS AND PEOPLE AROUND ME ARE GETTING HAZY...
I CAN'T FOCUS ON ANYTHING. THE WORLD IS IMMATERIAL...
NO MORE ROAD BUMPS, NO HIGHS, NO LOWS, EVERYTHING IS FLAT...
I CAN SPEND HOURS LOOKING AT A CRACK IN THE CEILING, BUT I CAN'T READ A BOOK MORE THAN A COUPLE OF SECONDS...
I DON'T KNOW IF EVERYONE ELSE IS TURNING INTO GHOSTS...
...OR IF IT'S ME WHO, LITTLE BY LITTLE, IS JUST TURNING INTO A SHADOW...
...SO INSUBSTANTIAL THAT I FEEL LIKE I'M FLOATING...
LIGHT...
SO LIGHT...

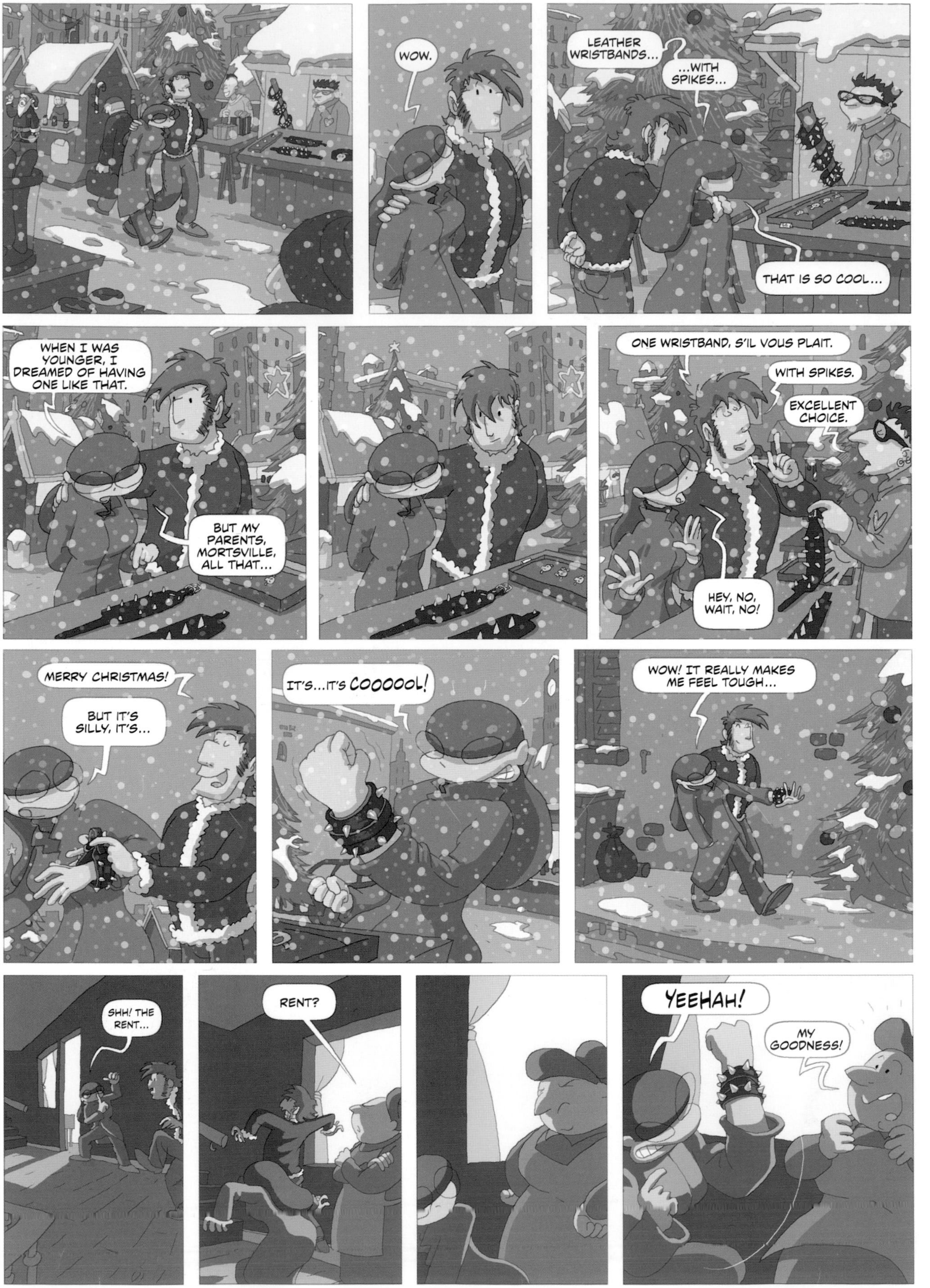
WOW.
LEATHER WRISTBANDS...
...WITH SPIKES...
THAT IS SO COOL...
WHEN I WAS YOUNGER, I DREAMED OF HAVING ONE LIKE THAT.
BUT MY PARENTS, MORTSVILLE, ALL THAT...
ONE WRISTBAND, S'IL VOUS PLAIT.
WITH SPIKES.
EXCELLENT CHOICE.
HEY, NO, WAIT, NO!
MERRY CHRISTMAS!
BUT IT'S SILLY, IT'S...
IT'S...IT'S COOOOOL!
WOW! IT REALLY MAKES ME FEEL TOUGH...
SHH! THE RENT...
RENT?
YEEHAH!
MY GOODNESS!

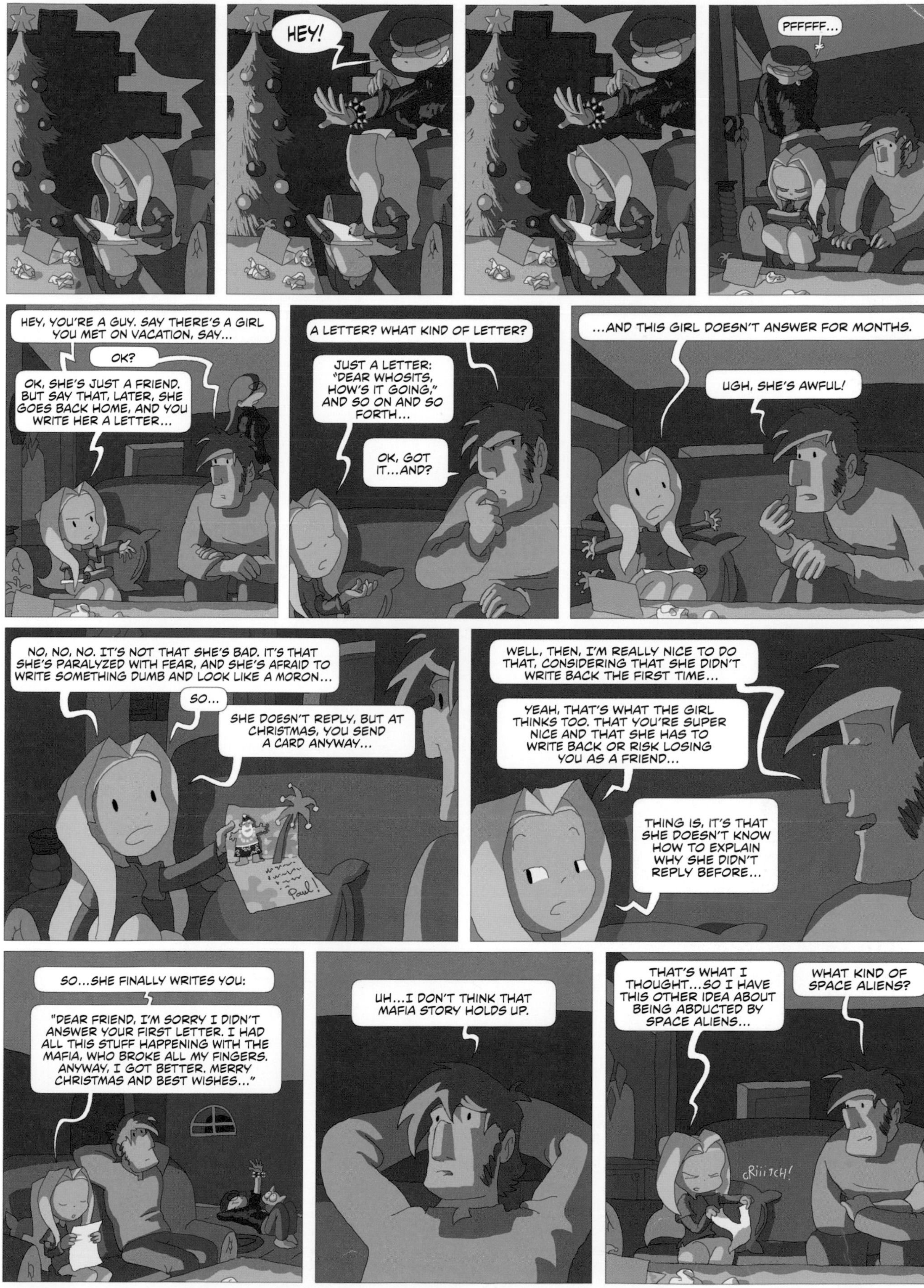

HEY!
PFFFFF...
HEY, YOU'RE A GUY. SAY THERE'S A GIRL YOU MET ON VACATION, SAY...
OK?
OK, SHE'S JUST A FRIEND. BUT SAY THAT, LATER, SHE GOES BACK HOME, AND YOU WRITE HER A LETTER...
A LETTER? WHAT KIND OF LETTER?
JUST A LETTER: "DEAR WHOSITS, HOW'S IT GOING," AND SO ON AND SO FORTH...
OK, GOT IT...AND?
...AND THIS GIRL DOESN'T ANSWER FOR MONTHS.
UGH, SHE'S AWFUL!
NO, NO, NO. IT'S NOT THAT SHE'S BAD. IT'S THAT SHE'S PARALYZED WITH FEAR, AND SHE'S AFRAID TO WRITE SOMETHING DUMB AND LOOK LIKE A MORON...
SO...
SHE DOESN'T REPLY, BUT AT CHRISTMAS, YOU SEND A CARD ANYWAY...
Paul!
WELL, THEN, I'M REALLY NICE TO DO THAT, CONSIDERING THAT SHE DIDN'T WRITE BACK THE FIRST TIME...
YEAH, THAT'S WHAT THE GIRL THINKS TOO. THAT YOU'RE SUPER NICE AND THAT SHE HAS TO WRITE BACK OR RISK LOSING YOU AS A FRIEND...
THING IS, IT'S THAT SHE DOESN'T KNOW HOW TO EXPLAIN WHY SHE DIDN'T REPLY BEFORE...
SO...SHE FINALLY WRITES YOU:
"DEAR FRIEND, I'M SORRY I DIDN'T ANSWER YOUR FIRST LETTER. I HAD ALL THIS STUFF HAPPENING WITH THE MAFIA, WHO BROKE ALL MY FINGERS. ANYWAY, I GOT BETTER. MERRY CHRISTMAS AND BEST WISHES..."
UH...I DON'T THINK THAT MAFIA STORY HOLDS UP.
THAT'S WHAT I THOUGHT...SO I HAVE THIS OTHER IDEA ABOUT BEING ABDUCTED BY SPACE ALIENS...
WHAT KIND OF SPACE ALIENS?
cRiiiTCH!

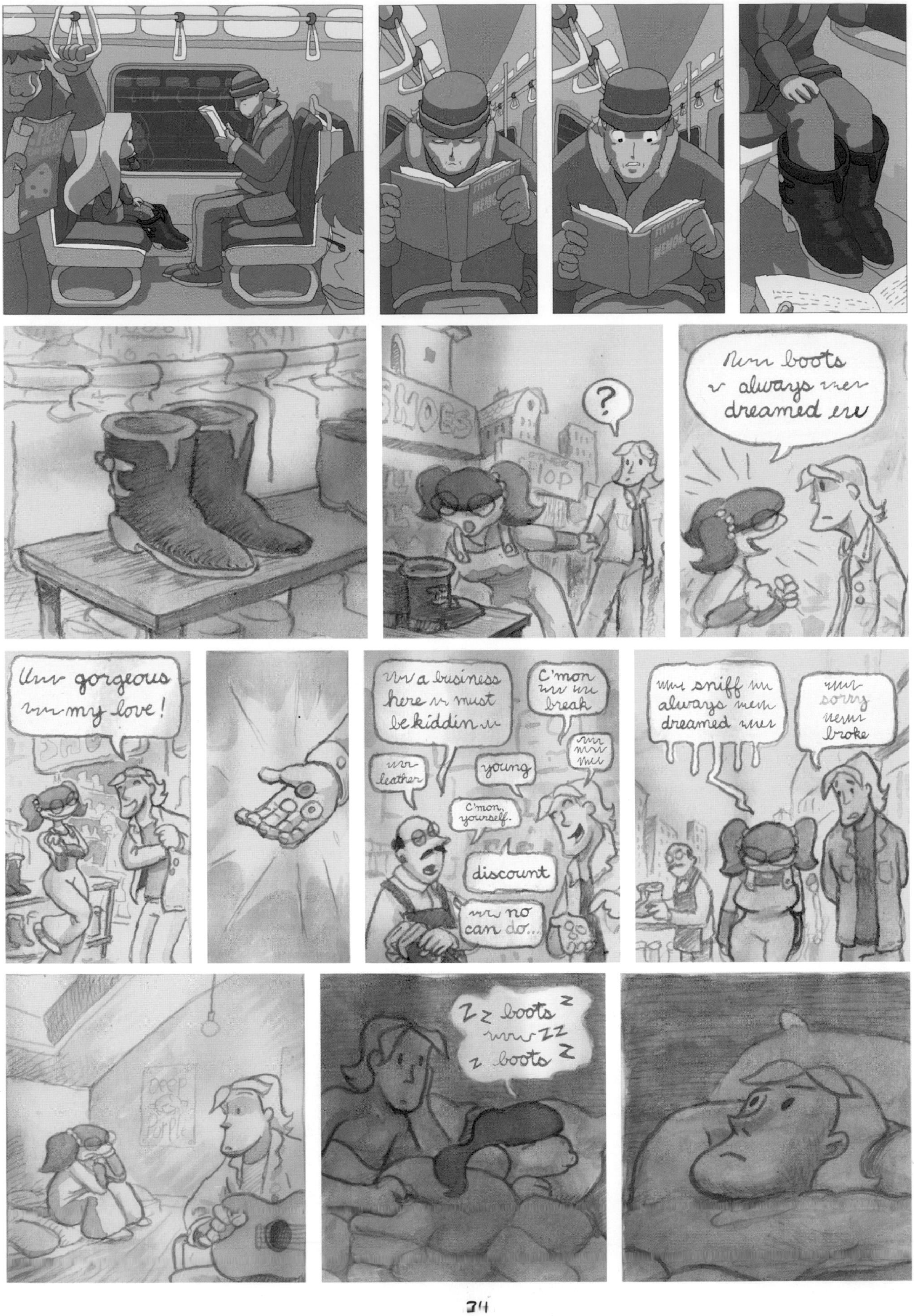
SHOES
SHOP
?
boots always dreamed
gorgeous my love!
a business here must be kiddin
C'mon break
leather
young
C'mon, yourself.
discount
no can do...
sniff always dreamed
sorry broke
Z z boots z
zz
z boots z

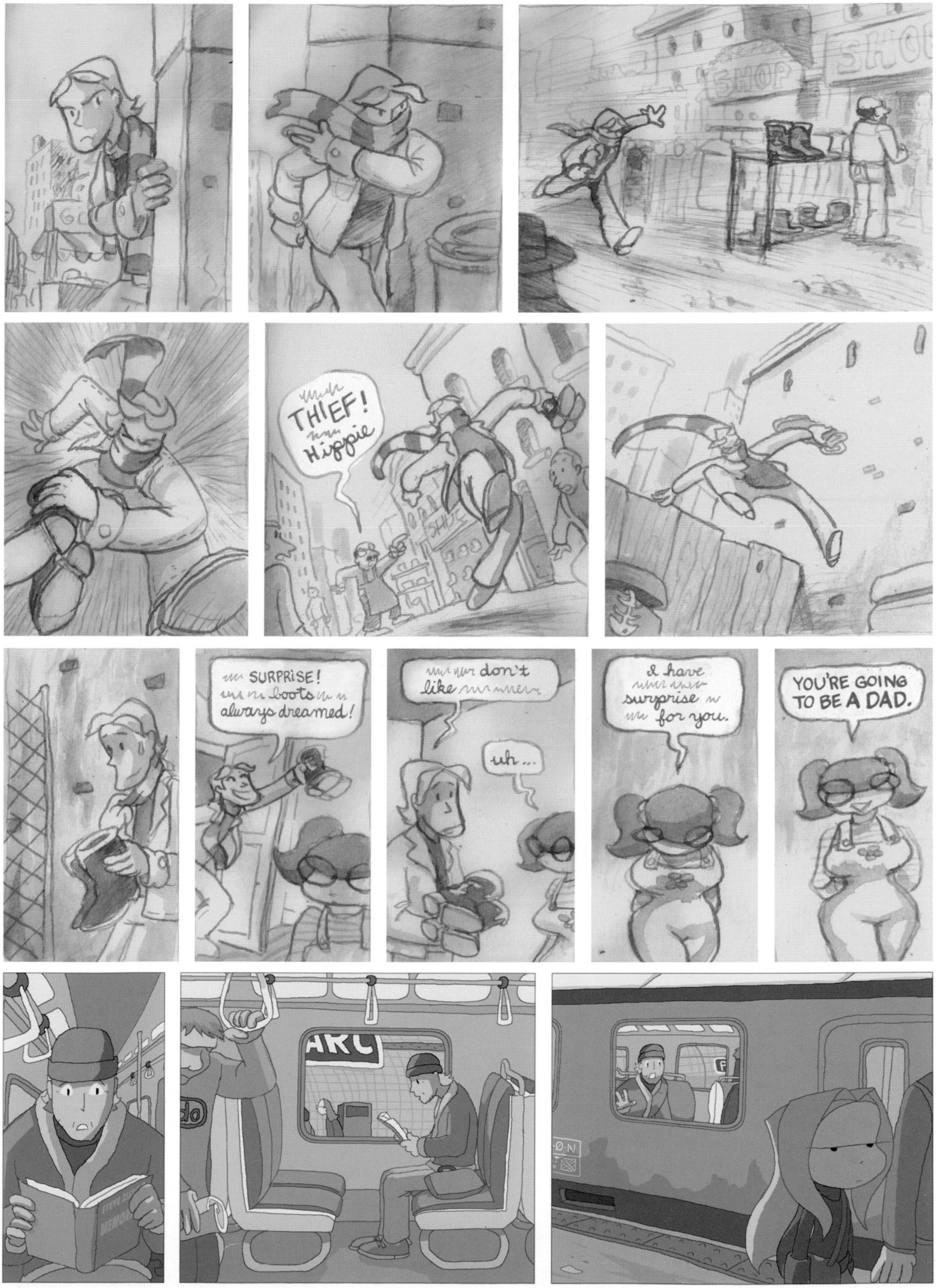
THIEF!
Hippie
SURPRISE!
boots
always dreamed!
don't
like
uh...
I have
surprise
for you.
YOU'RE GOING TO BE A DAD.
ARC

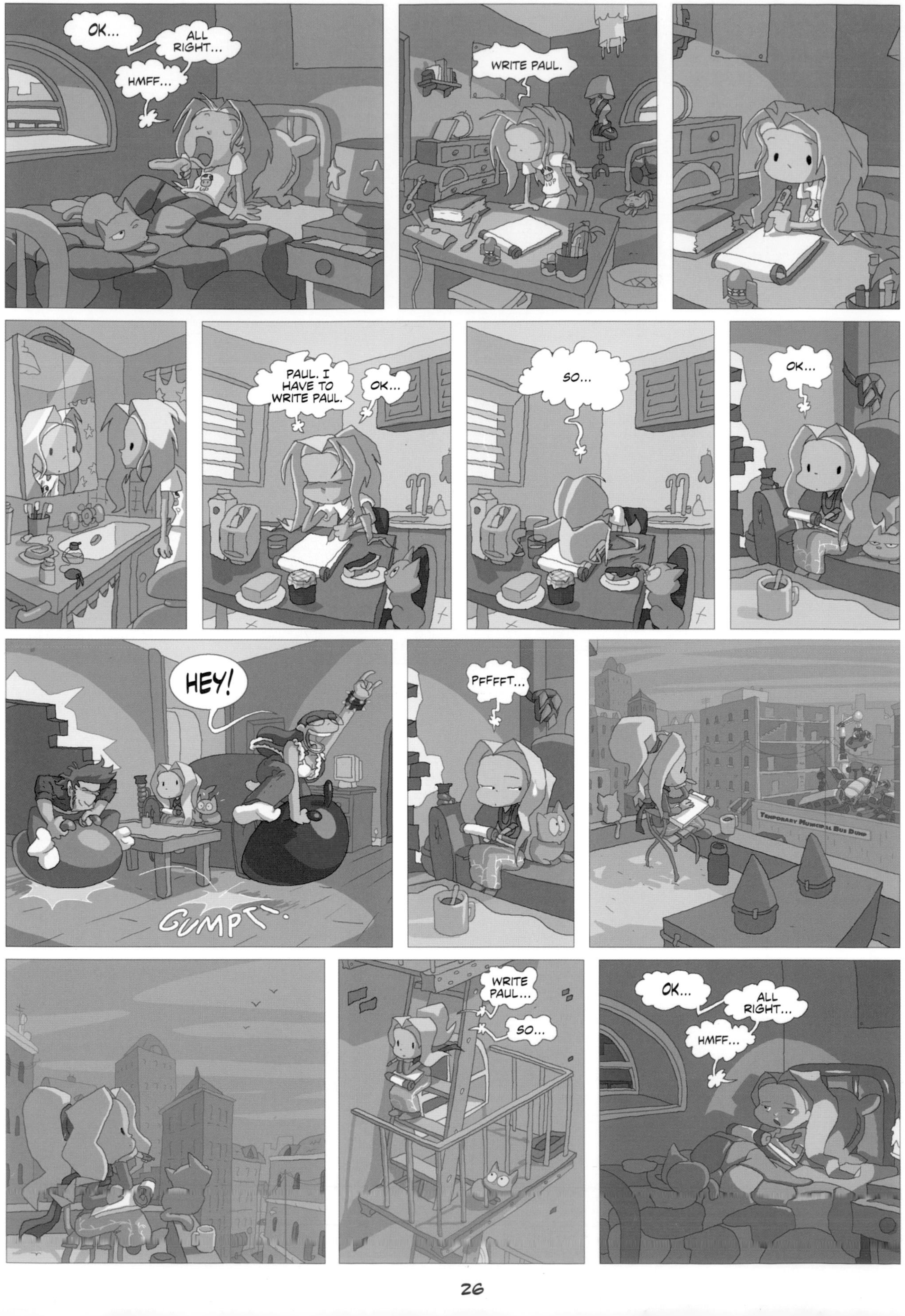
OK...
ALL RIGHT...
HMFF...
WRITE PAUL.
PAUL. I HAVE TO WRITE PAUL.
OK...
SO...
OK...
HEY!
GUMPT
PFFFFT...
TEMPORARY MUNICIPAL BUS DUMP
WRITE PAUL...
SO...
OK...
ALL RIGHT...
HMFF...

HEY.

WHAT?

NEXT PERIOD.

YEAH?

WE'RE CUTTING.

HUH? OH, UH...

OK, SURE.

I KNOW A GOOD HIDEOUT.

The Black Darkness Goth Café

ESPRESSO.

UH...ME TOO.

SO, YOU KNOW THAT BOY, PAUL, I TOLD YOU ABOUT? HE WROTE ME, AND I HAVEN'T WRITTEN BACK YET.

YEAH, YEAH, Y'KNOW, GUYS ARE ALL THE SAME...

FOR EXAMPLE, I BROKE UP WITH THAT GUY WHO DOES HENNA TATTOOS, HE WAS ALWAYS FREAKING OUT ABOUT STUFF, LIKE I CARE ABOUT HIS LITTLE PROBLEMS. Y'KNOW, IF YOU LOOK AT WHAT'S GOING ON IN THE WORLD, IT'LL TOTALLY MESS YOU UP...

IT'S LIKE AMERICANS THINK WE'RE THE MASTERS OF THE WORLD, WHEN WE'RE REALLY SELLING WEAPONS FOR OIL, BUT IN THE END ALL GOVERNMENTS ARE ALL COMPLETE FAKE LIARS...

AND, Y'KNOW, I CAN'T STAND INJUSTICE, EVEN MORE THAN POVERTY, FRANKLY, SO I DON'T WANT TO GO TO WORK AT SOME FACTORY LIKE A SHEEP, Y'KNOW. AND THAT'S WHAT GETS ALL UP IN THE MAN'S FACE, BECAUSE I WON'T BE A PART OF THE SYSTEM...

SHUT UP!

UM...

I... I...

The Black Darkness Goth Café

KSHLUNK
KSHLUNK

BiP BiP
BiP

HELLO?

MOM?

HELLOOOO?

WHAT DO YOU MEAN, YOU CAN'T HEAR?

TURN IT AROUND!

HOLD THE PHONE THE OTHER SIDE UP!

IT'S WORKING?

YOU OK?

GOOD.

RIGHT, THE ARTHRITIS.

YES, YES.

YES, IT'S A PAIN, YES.

YES, THAT TOO, YES.

AND THE VARICOSE VEINS, OF COURSE...

YOU SAW THE DOCTOR?

OF COURSE I REMEMBER CLEMENT FIFFER...

HUH?

WE'RE NOT GOING BACK OVER THAT AGAIN, ARE WE?

YEAH, YEAH SO, YOU KNOW MY BOOK THAT I WROTE...?

...WELL, IT CAME OUT.

YES.

HUH?

I DON'T CARE THAT MRS. BIGGINS'S GRANDSON GOT HIS ENGINEERING DEGREE!

I WROTE A BOOK GOSHDARNIT!

FINE, THEN CONGRATULATE HER FOR ME!

BYE!

BiP.

RAAAAAAAAAAAAAAA

PWOF

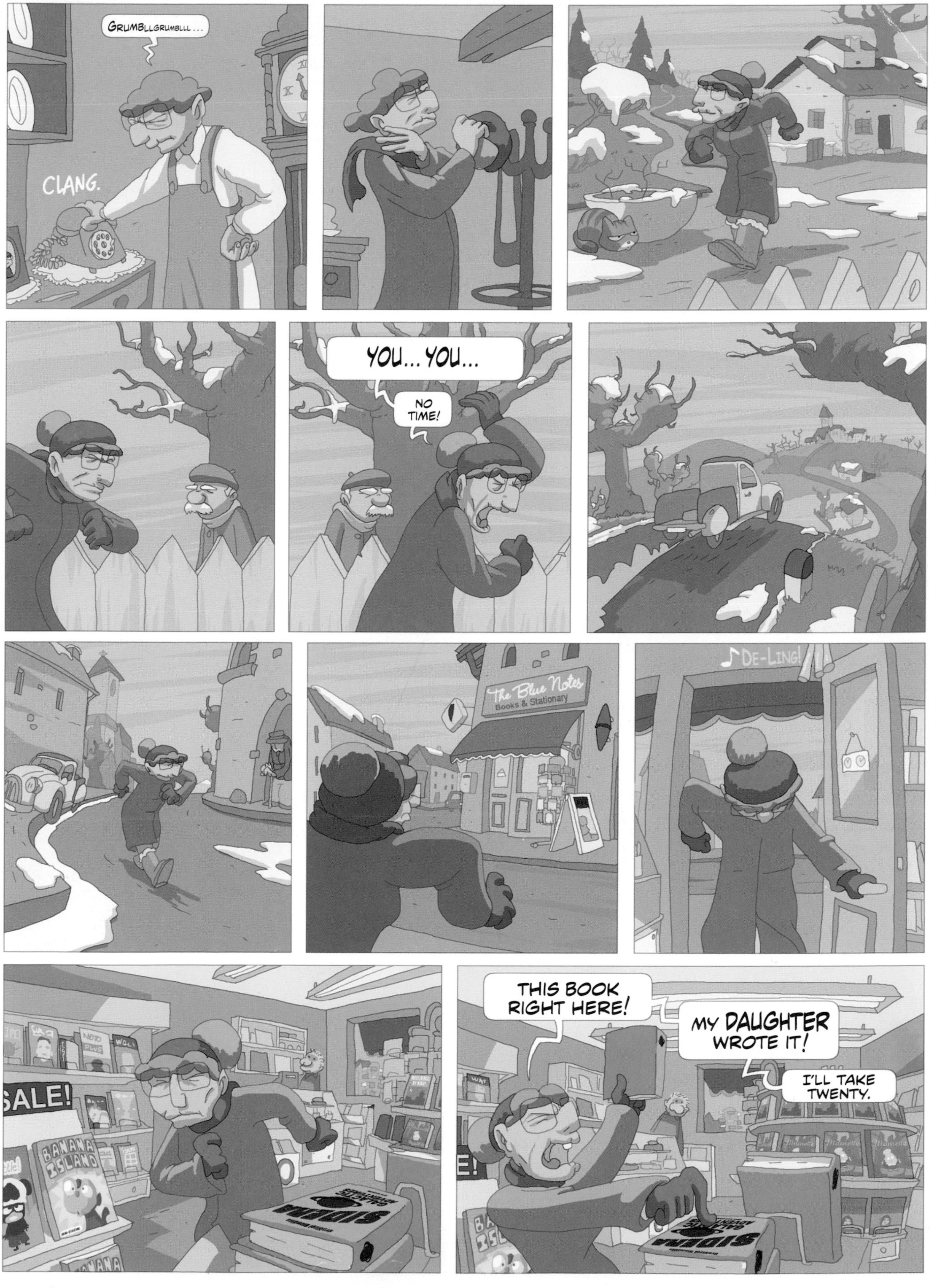
GRUMBLLGRUMBLLL...
CLANG.
YOU... YOU...
NO TIME!
The Blue Notes
Books & Stationary
DE-LING!
SALE!
BANANA ISLAND
THIS BOOK RIGHT HERE!
MY DAUGHTER WROTE IT!
I'LL TAKE TWENTY.

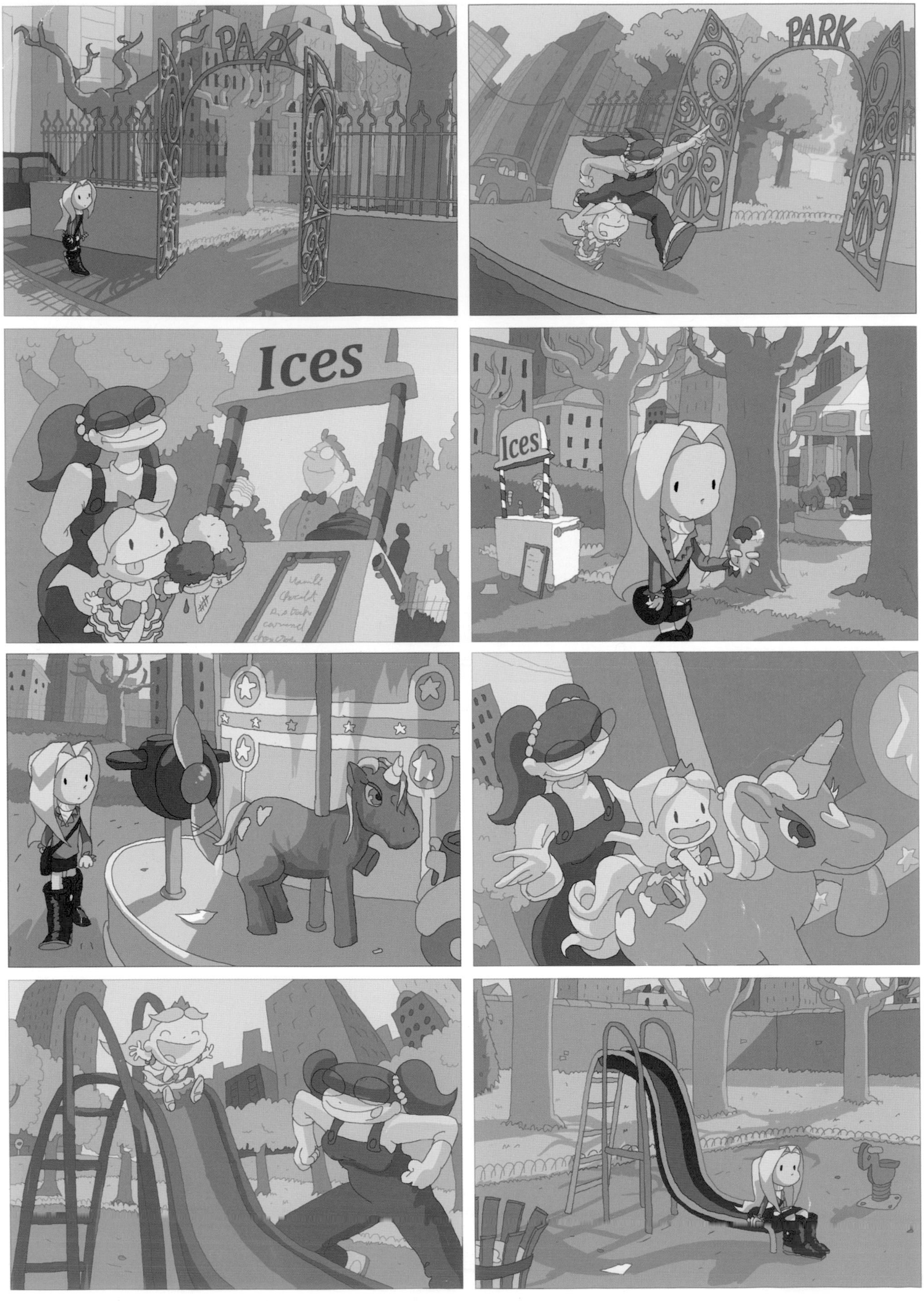
PARK
PARK
Ices
Ices

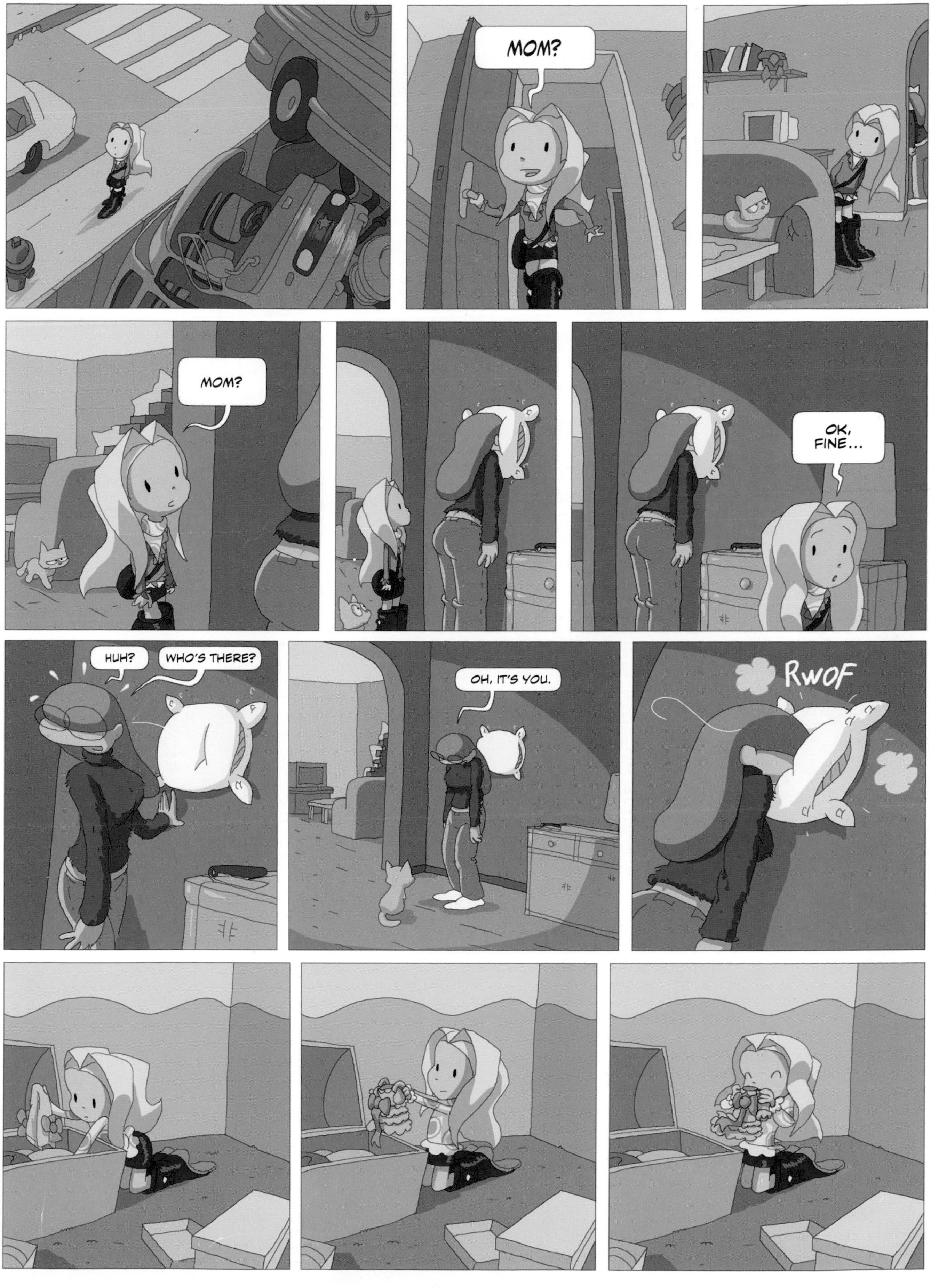
MOM?
MOM?
OK, FINE...
HUH?
WHO'S THERE?
OH, IT'S YOU.
RWOF

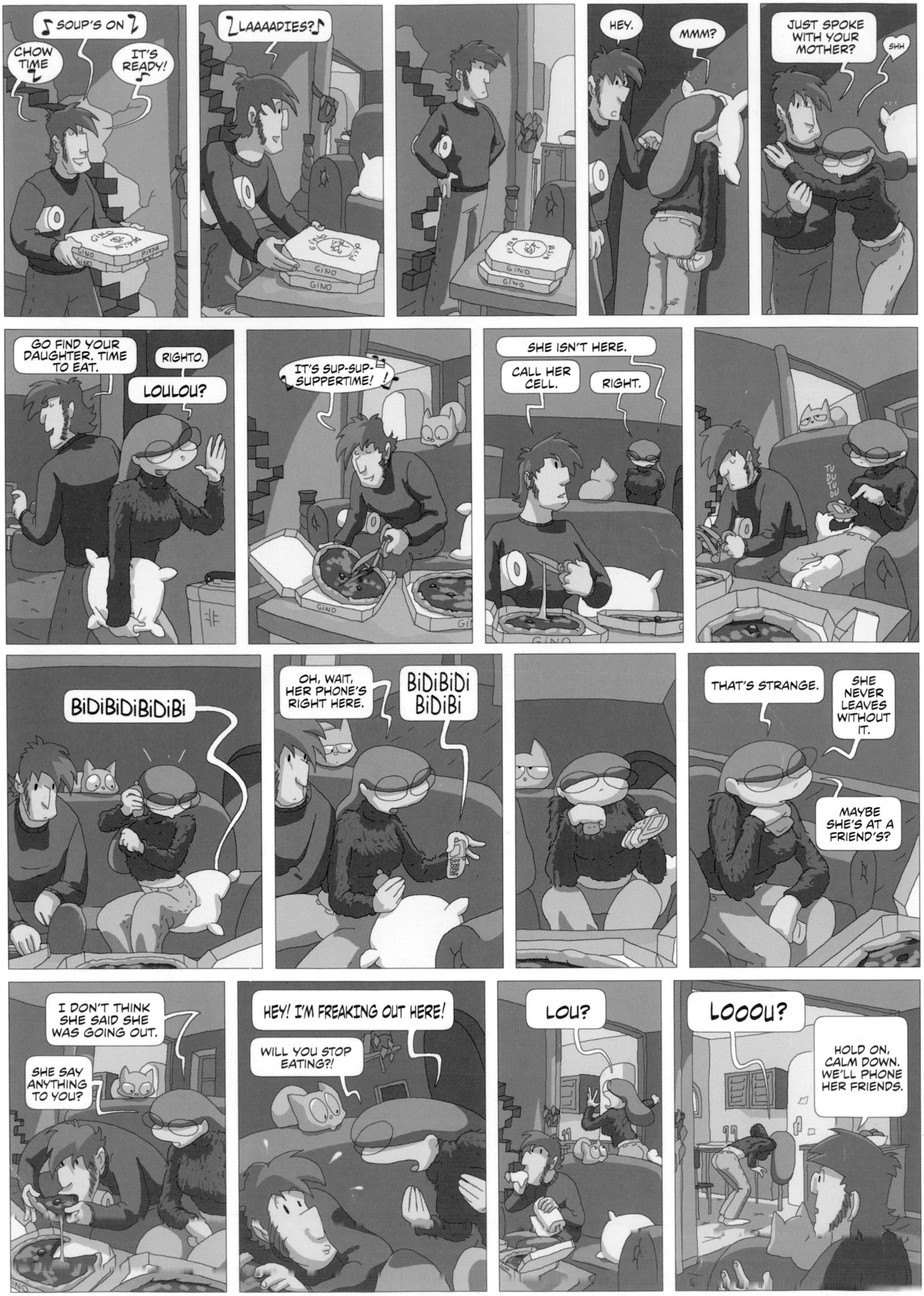
SOUP'S ON
CHOW TIME
IT'S READY!
GINO PIZZA
LAAAADIES?
HEY.
MMM?
JUST SPOKE WITH YOUR MOTHER?
SHH
GO FIND YOUR DAUGHTER. TIME TO EAT.
RIGHTO.
LOULOU?
IT'S SUP-SUP-SUPPERTIME!
SHE ISN'T HERE.
CALL HER CELL.
RIGHT.
TU DU TU DU
BiDiBiDiBiDiBi
OH, WAIT, HER PHONE'S RIGHT HERE.
BiDiBiDi BiDiBi
THAT'S STRANGE.
SHE NEVER LEAVES WITHOUT IT.
MAYBE SHE'S AT A FRIEND'S?
I DON'T THINK SHE SAID SHE WAS GOING OUT.
SHE SAY ANYTHING TO YOU?
HEY! I'M FREAKING OUT HERE!
WILL YOU STOP EATING?!
LOU?
LOOOU?
HOLD ON, CALM DOWN. WE'LL PHONE HER FRIENDS.

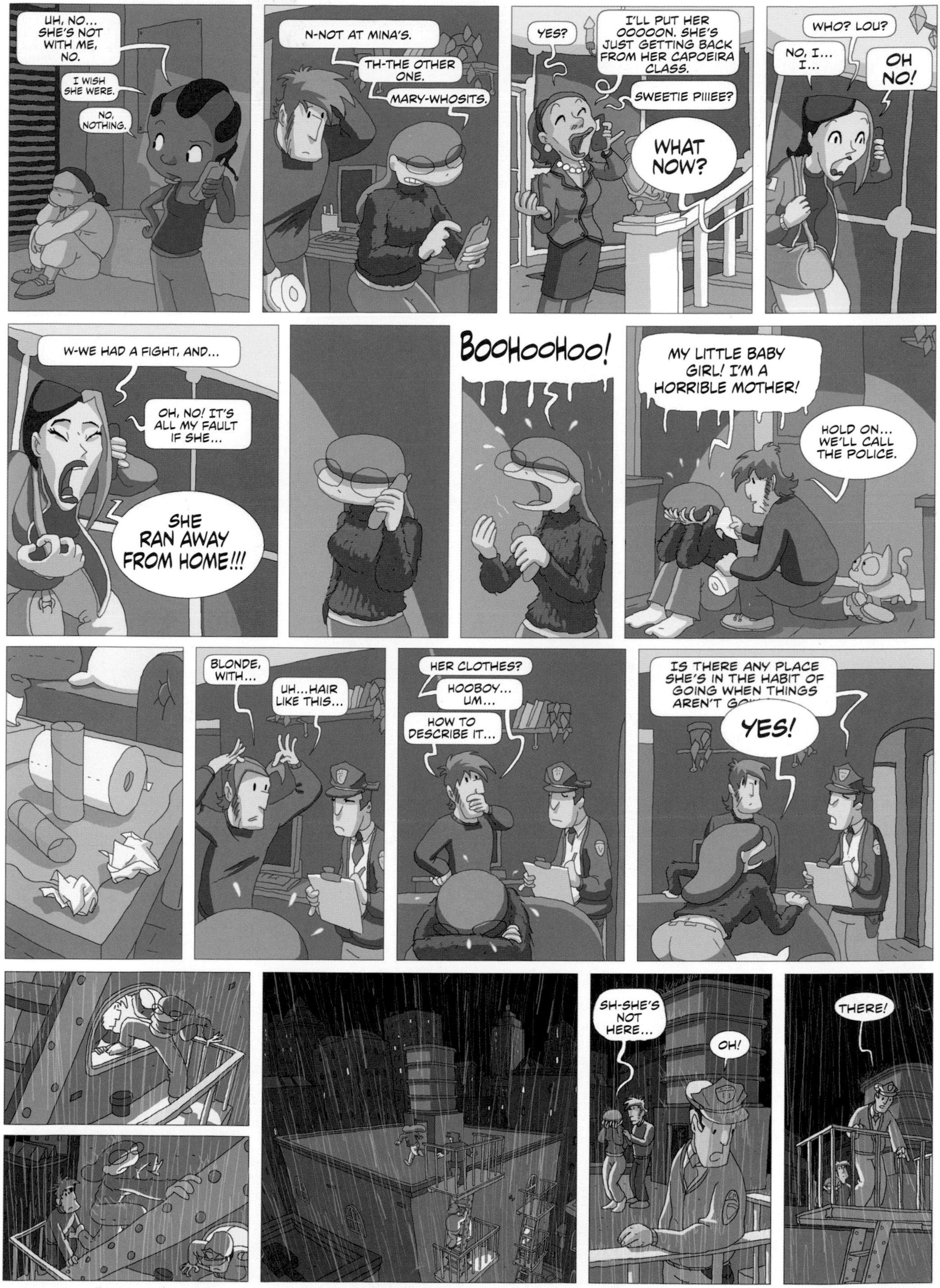
UH, NO... SHE'S NOT WITH ME, NO.
I WISH SHE WERE.
NO, NOTHING.
N-NOT AT MINA'S.
TH-THE OTHER ONE.
MARY-WHOSITS.
YES?
I'LL PUT HER OOOOON. SHE'S JUST GETTING BACK FROM HER CAPOEIRA CLASS.
SWEETIE PIIIEE?
WHAT NOW?
WHO? LOU?
NO, I... I...
OH NO!
W-WE HAD A FIGHT, AND...
OH, NO! IT'S ALL MY FAULT IF SHE...
SHE RAN AWAY FROM HOME!!!
BOOHOOHOO!
MY LITTLE BABY GIRL! I'M A HORRIBLE MOTHER!
HOLD ON... WE'LL CALL THE POLICE.
BLONDE, WITH...
UH...HAIR LIKE THIS...
HER CLOTHES?
HOOBOY... UM...
HOW TO DESCRIBE IT...
IS THERE ANY PLACE SHE'S IN THE HABIT OF GOING WHEN THINGS AREN'T GO
YES!
SH-SHE'S NOT HERE...
OH!
THERE!

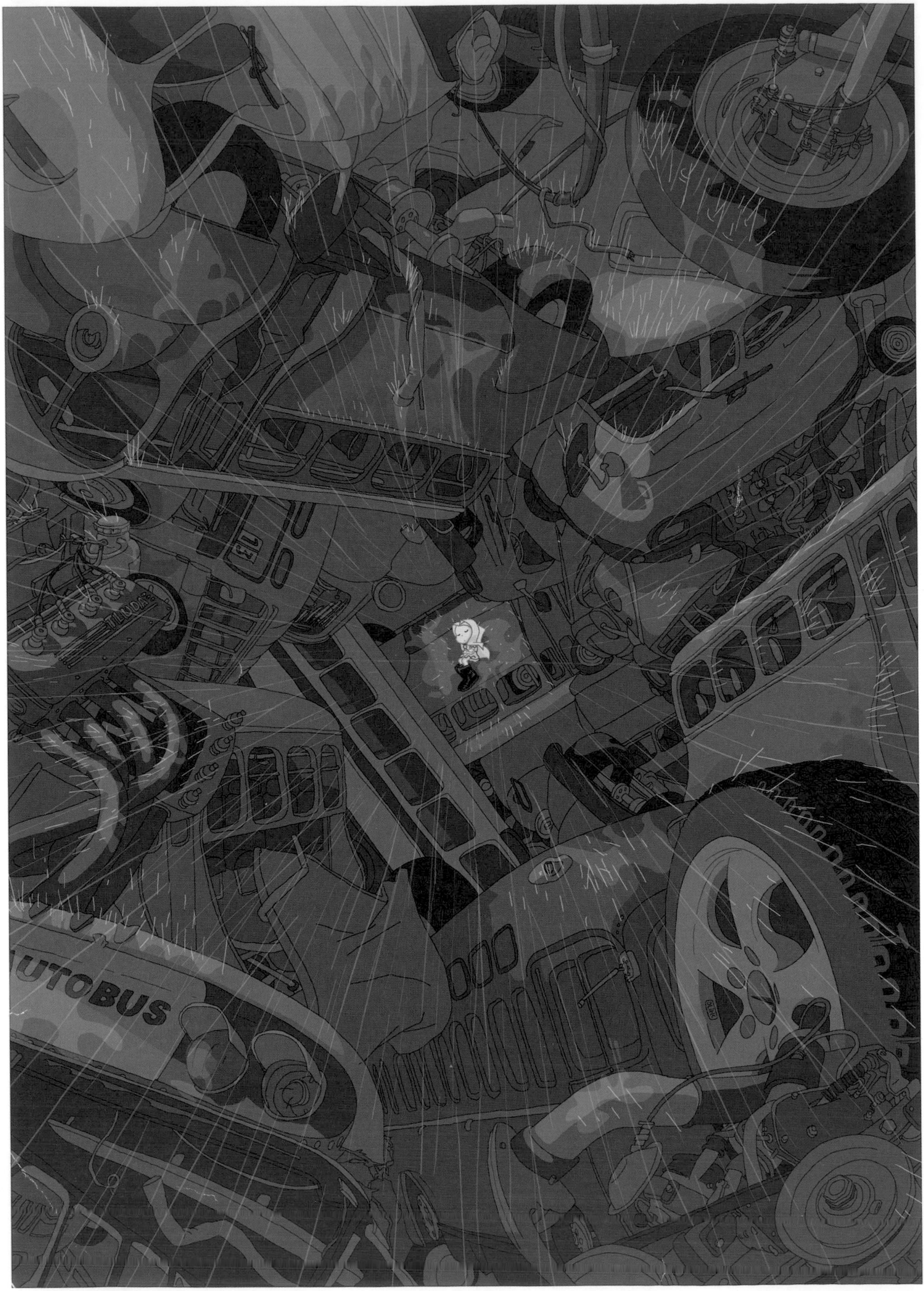
UTOBUS

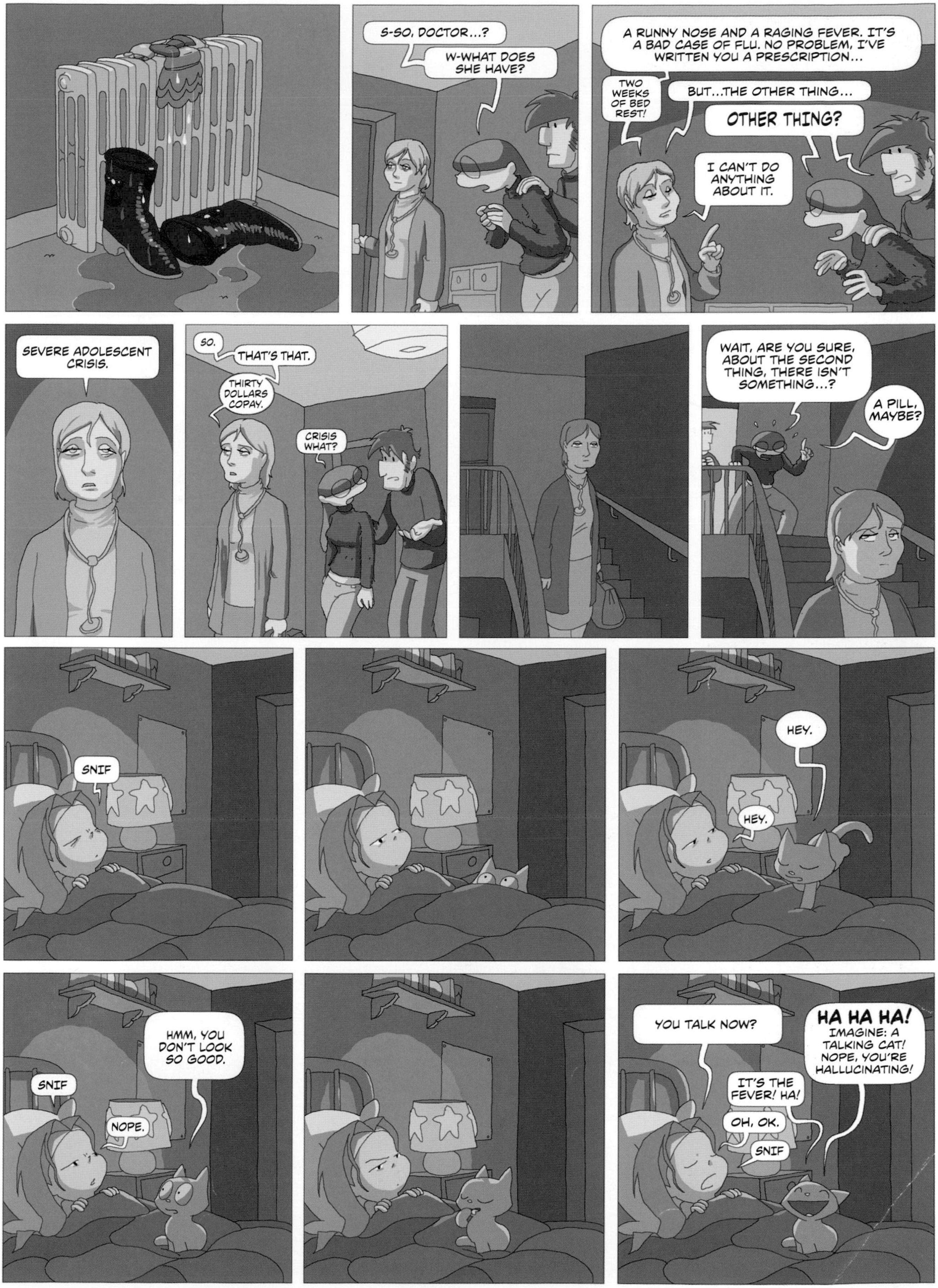
S-SO, DOCTOR...?
W-WHAT DOES SHE HAVE?
A RUNNY NOSE AND A RAGING FEVER. IT'S A BAD CASE OF FLU. NO PROBLEM, I'VE WRITTEN YOU A PRESCRIPTION...
TWO WEEKS OF BED REST!
BUT...THE OTHER THING...
OTHER THING?
I CAN'T DO ANYTHING ABOUT IT.
SEVERE ADOLESCENT CRISIS.
SO.
THAT'S THAT.
THIRTY DOLLARS COPAY.
CRISIS WHAT?
WAIT, ARE YOU SURE, ABOUT THE SECOND THING, THERE ISN'T SOMETHING...?
A PILL, MAYBE?
SNIF
HEY.
HEY.
HMM, YOU DON'T LOOK SO GOOD.
SNIF
NOPE.
YOU TALK NOW?
HA HA HA! IMAGINE: A TALKING CAT! NOPE, YOU'RE HALLUCINATING!
IT'S THE FEVER! HA!
OH, OK.
SNIF

CAN I GET UNDER THE COVERS?

MAKE YOURSELF AT HOME...

OOH, IT'S WARM!

SNIF

HEHE!

HOLD ON, I'M COMING IN.

MMMM.

I NEVER WANT TO COME OUT FROM HERE.

YOU AND ME BOTH.

ALL CURLED UP COMFY?

TOTALLY.

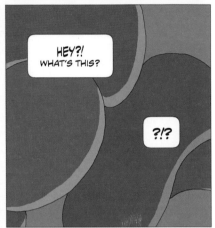

HEY?! WHAT'S THIS?

?!?

WHOA?!?

WHAT'S GOING ON HERE?!

HUH? NO, I...

♪ LOU NEEDS A TRAINING BRA! ♪

SHHHH! SOMEONE'LL HEAR YOU!

HEY, THERE'S NOTHING WRONG WITH, Y'KNOW, DEVELOPING!

NOTHING WRONG, BUT IT FREAKS ME OUT A LITTLE.

SNIF

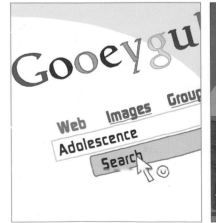

Gooeygu

Web   Images   Group

Adolescence

Search

O...M...G!

WHAA?

WHAAAA?

WHAAAA?

LOOK AT THAT PICTURE...

WHAAAAA?

THIS IS BAD.

HOW DID THIS HAPPEN? HOW DID THIS HAPPEN? I...I DIDN'T SEE IT COMING...JUST YESTERDAY SHE WAS SO LITTLE, AND THEN...WHAM!

TEENAGER.

I'M A TOTAL FAILURE, EVER SINCE SHE WAS A BABY. BUT I TRIED TO DO EVERYTHING RIGHT. MAKE SURE SHE NEVER WANTED FOR ANYTHING, THAT SHE WAS HAPPY...AND...

I, UH...I DON'T KNOW...RAISING A KID, IT'S, UM...LIKE STAR WARS...JEDI TRAINING...SO, YOU HAVE TO BE LIKE OBI-WAN, AND SHE'S LIKE ANAKIN...

HUH?

OH, NO, WAIT: YOU'RE YODA, AND...

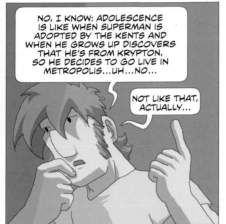

NO, I KNOW: ADOLESCENCE IS LIKE WHEN SUPERMAN IS ADOPTED BY THE KENTS AND WHEN HE GROWS UP DISCOVERS THAT HE'S FROM KRYPTON, SO HE DECIDES TO GO LIVE IN METROPOLIS...UH...NO...

NOT LIKE THAT, ACTUALLY...

I DON'T THINK I'M THE RIGHT PERSON TO TALK ABOUT THIS STUFF. ALL I'VE GOT ARE MY STUPID SUPERHERO STORIES...UH...I THINK THAT, AS A MOM, YOU'RE AWESOME. LOU IS BRIGHT AND CREATIVE, AND NOW THAT SHE'S A TEENAGER, OF COURSE THERE'S GONNA BE STUFF YOU DON'T UNDERSTAND...

...AND THIS IS A JOURNEY SHE HAS TO TAKE ON HER OWN.

...I BELIEVE.

YOU'RE NICE.

BUT BACK TO STAR WARS. I'D BE MORE LIKE QUI-GON JINN, RIGHT?

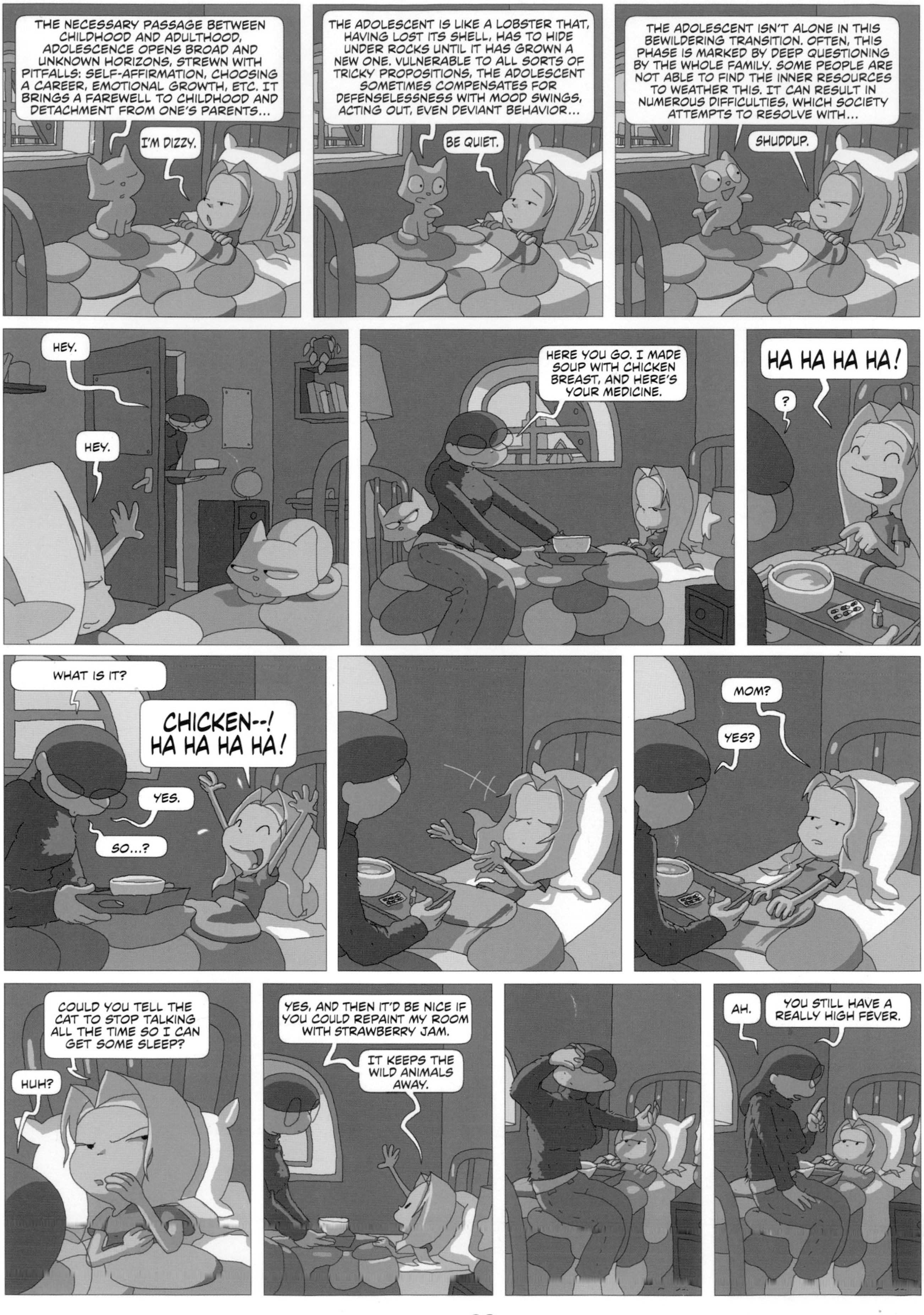

THE NECESSARY PASSAGE BETWEEN CHILDHOOD AND ADULTHOOD, ADOLESCENCE OPENS BROAD AND UNKNOWN HORIZONS, STREWN WITH PITFALLS: SELF-AFFIRMATION, CHOOSING A CAREER, EMOTIONAL GROWTH, ETC. IT BRINGS A FAREWELL TO CHILDHOOD AND DETACHMENT FROM ONE'S PARENTS...
I'M DIZZY.
THE ADOLESCENT IS LIKE A LOBSTER THAT, HAVING LOST ITS SHELL, HAS TO HIDE UNDER ROCKS UNTIL IT HAS GROWN A NEW ONE. VULNERABLE TO ALL SORTS OF TRICKY PROPOSITIONS, THE ADOLESCENT SOMETIMES COMPENSATES FOR DEFENSELESSNESS WITH MOOD SWINGS, ACTING OUT, EVEN DEVIANT BEHAVIOR...
BE QUIET.
THE ADOLESCENT ISN'T ALONE IN THIS BEWILDERING TRANSITION. OFTEN, THIS PHASE IS MARKED BY DEEP QUESTIONING BY THE WHOLE FAMILY. SOME PEOPLE ARE NOT ABLE TO FIND THE INNER RESOURCES TO WEATHER THIS. IT CAN RESULT IN NUMEROUS DIFFICULTIES, WHICH SOCIETY ATTEMPTS TO RESOLVE WITH...
SHUDDUP.
HEY.
HEY.
HERE YOU GO. I MADE SOUP WITH CHICKEN BREAST, AND HERE'S YOUR MEDICINE.
HA HA HA HA!
?
WHAT IS IT?
CHICKEN--! HA HA HA HA!
YES.
SO...?
MOM?
YES?
COULD YOU TELL THE CAT TO STOP TALKING ALL THE TIME SO I CAN GET SOME SLEEP?
HUH?
YES, AND THEN IT'D BE NICE IF YOU COULD REPAINT MY ROOM WITH STRAWBERRY JAM.
IT KEEPS THE WILD ANIMALS AWAY.
AH.
YOU STILL HAVE A REALLY HIGH FEVER.

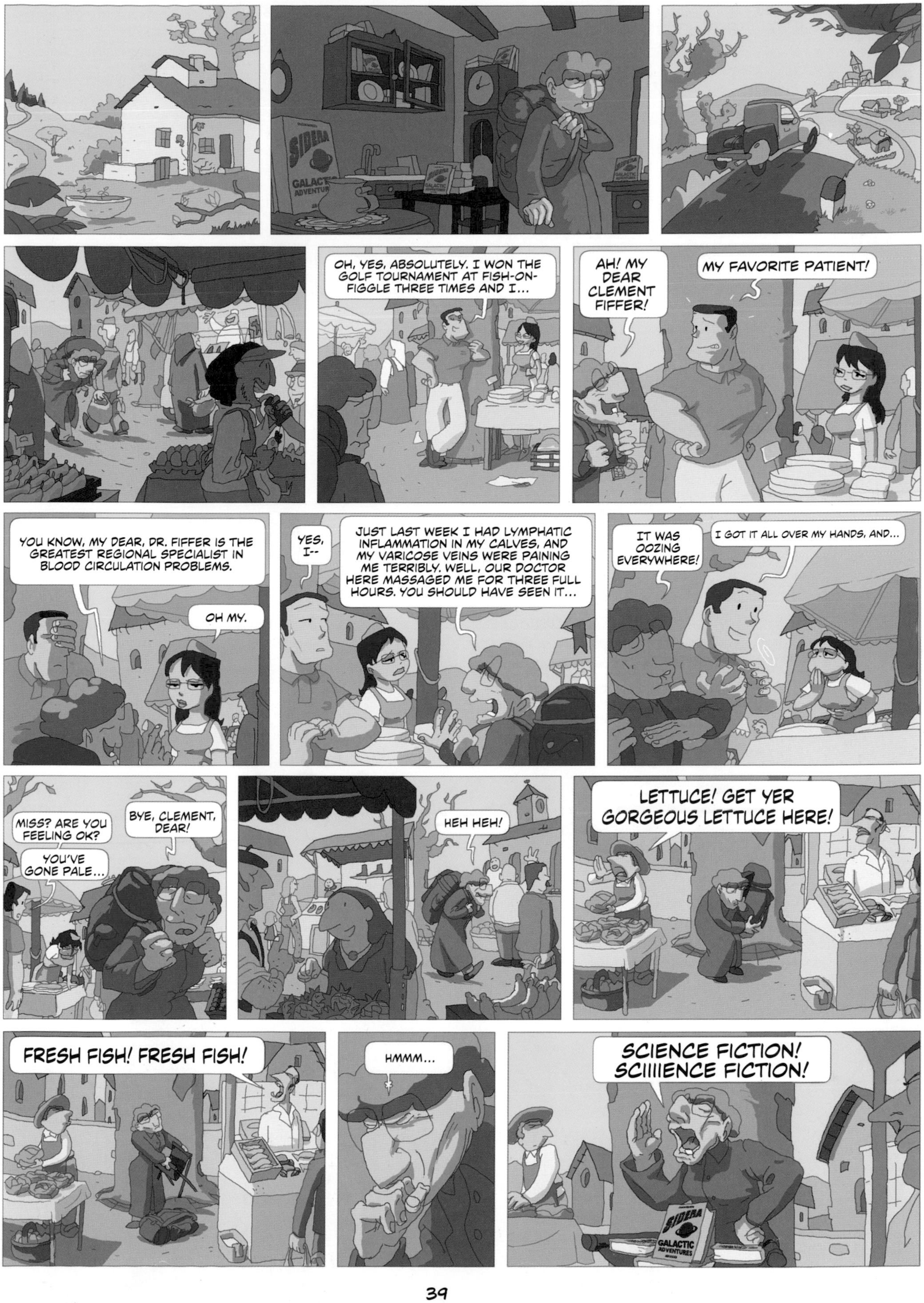
OH, YES, ABSOLUTELY. I WON THE GOLF TOURNAMENT AT FISH-ON-FIGGLE THREE TIMES AND I...
AH! MY DEAR CLEMENT FIFFER!
MY FAVORITE PATIENT!
YOU KNOW, MY DEAR, DR. FIFFER IS THE GREATEST REGIONAL SPECIALIST IN BLOOD CIRCULATION PROBLEMS.
OH MY.
YES, I--
JUST LAST WEEK I HAD LYMPHATIC INFLAMMATION IN MY CALVES, AND MY VARICOSE VEINS WERE PAINING ME TERRIBLY. WELL, OUR DOCTOR HERE MASSAGED ME FOR THREE FULL HOURS. YOU SHOULD HAVE SEEN IT...
IT WAS OOZING EVERYWHERE!
I GOT IT ALL OVER MY HANDS, AND...
MISS? ARE YOU FEELING OK?
YOU'VE GONE PALE...
BYE, CLEMENT, DEAR!
HEH HEH!
LETTUCE! GET YER GORGEOUS LETTUCE HERE!
FRESH FISH! FRESH FISH!
HMMM...
SCIENCE FICTION! SCIIIIENCE FICTION!

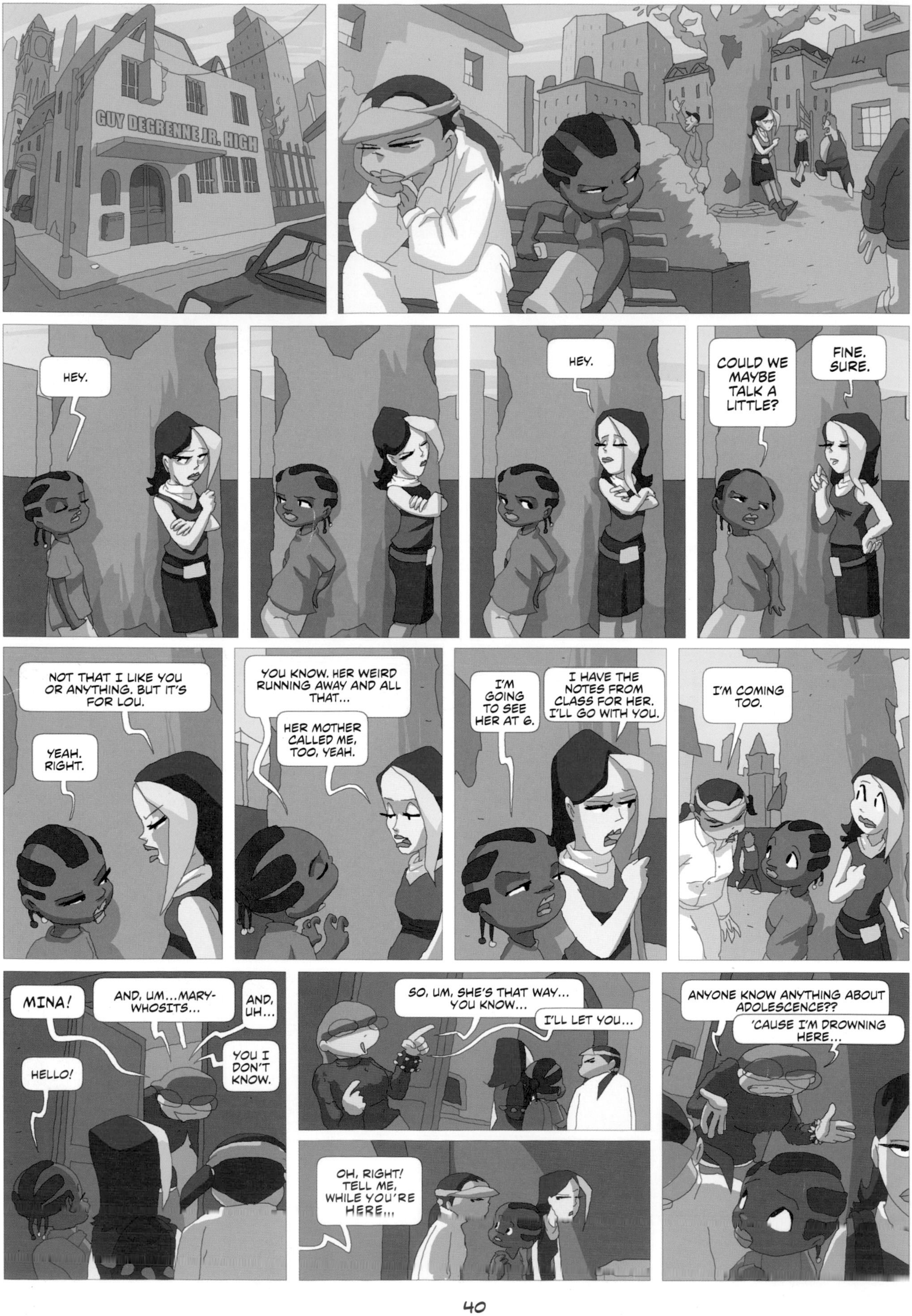
GUY DEGRENNE JR. HIGH
HEY.
HEY.
COULD WE MAYBE TALK A LITTLE?
FINE. SURE.
NOT THAT I LIKE YOU OR ANYTHING. BUT IT'S FOR LOU.
YEAH. RIGHT.
YOU KNOW. HER WEIRD RUNNING AWAY AND ALL THAT...
HER MOTHER CALLED ME, TOO, YEAH.
I'M GOING TO SEE HER AT 6.
I HAVE THE NOTES FROM CLASS FOR HER. I'LL GO WITH YOU.
I'M COMING TOO.
MINA!
HELLO!
AND, UM...MARY-WHOSITS...
AND, UH...
YOU I DON'T KNOW.
SO, UM, SHE'S THAT WAY... YOU KNOW...
I'LL LET YOU...
OH, RIGHT! TELL ME, WHILE YOU'RE HERE...
ANYONE KNOW ANYTHING ABOUT ADOLESCENCE??
'CAUSE I'M DROWNING HERE...

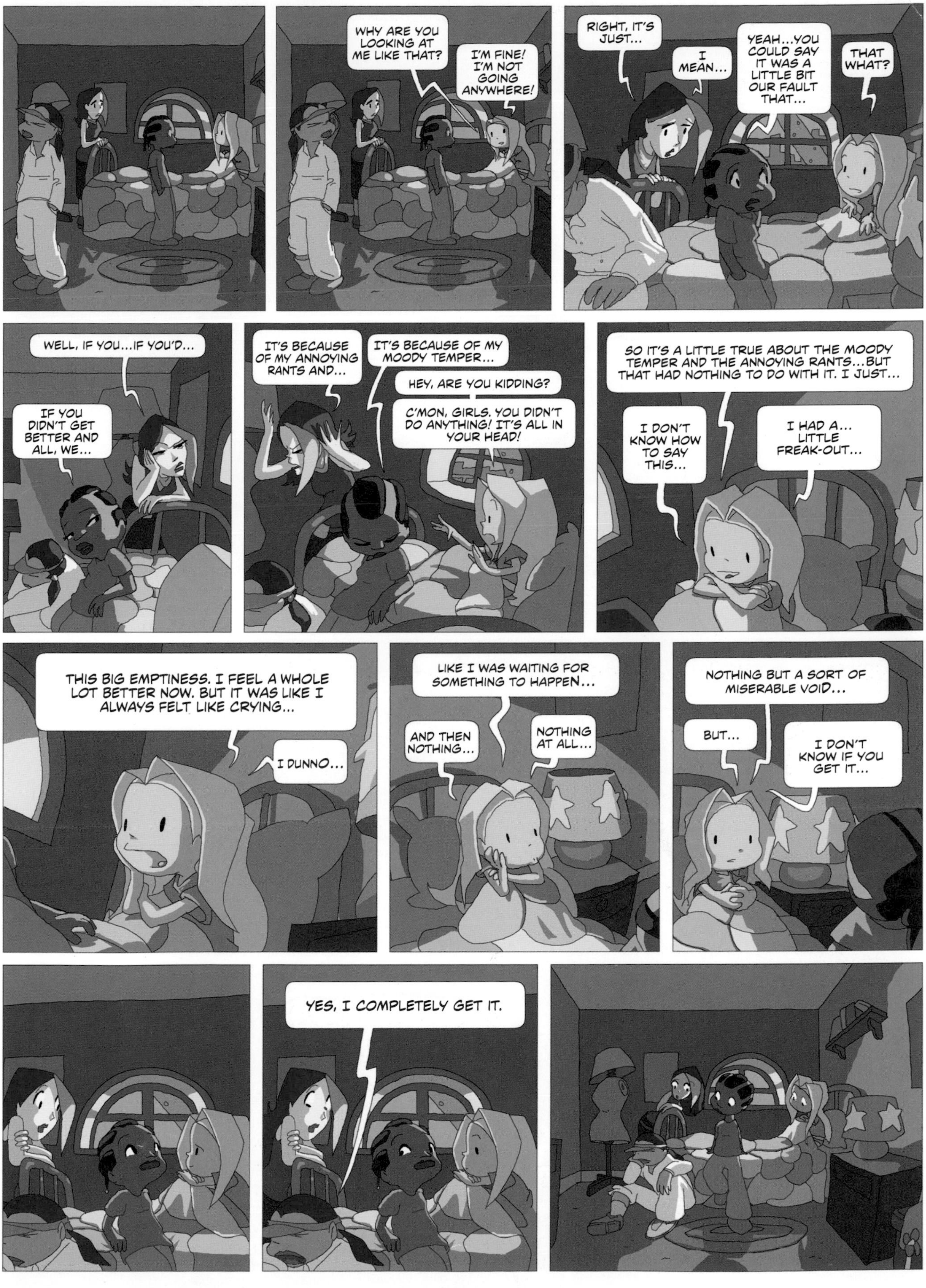

WHY ARE YOU LOOKING AT ME LIKE THAT?
I'M FINE! I'M NOT GOING ANYWHERE!
RIGHT, IT'S JUST...
I MEAN...
YEAH...YOU COULD SAY IT WAS A LITTLE BIT OUR FAULT THAT...
THAT WHAT?
WELL, IF YOU...IF YOU'D...
IF YOU DIDN'T GET BETTER AND ALL, WE...
IT'S BECAUSE OF MY ANNOYING RANTS AND...
IT'S BECAUSE OF MY MOODY TEMPER...
HEY, ARE YOU KIDDING?
C'MON, GIRLS. YOU DIDN'T DO ANYTHING! IT'S ALL IN YOUR HEAD!
SO IT'S A LITTLE TRUE ABOUT THE MOODY TEMPER AND THE ANNOYING RANTS...BUT THAT HAD NOTHING TO DO WITH IT. I JUST...
I DON'T KNOW HOW TO SAY THIS...
I HAD A... LITTLE FREAK-OUT...
THIS BIG EMPTINESS. I FEEL A WHOLE LOT BETTER NOW. BUT IT WAS LIKE I ALWAYS FELT LIKE CRYING...
I DUNNO...
LIKE I WAS WAITING FOR SOMETHING TO HAPPEN...
AND THEN NOTHING...
NOTHING AT ALL...
NOTHING BUT A SORT OF MISERABLE VOID...
BUT...
I DON'T KNOW IF YOU GET IT...
YES, I COMPLETELY GET IT.

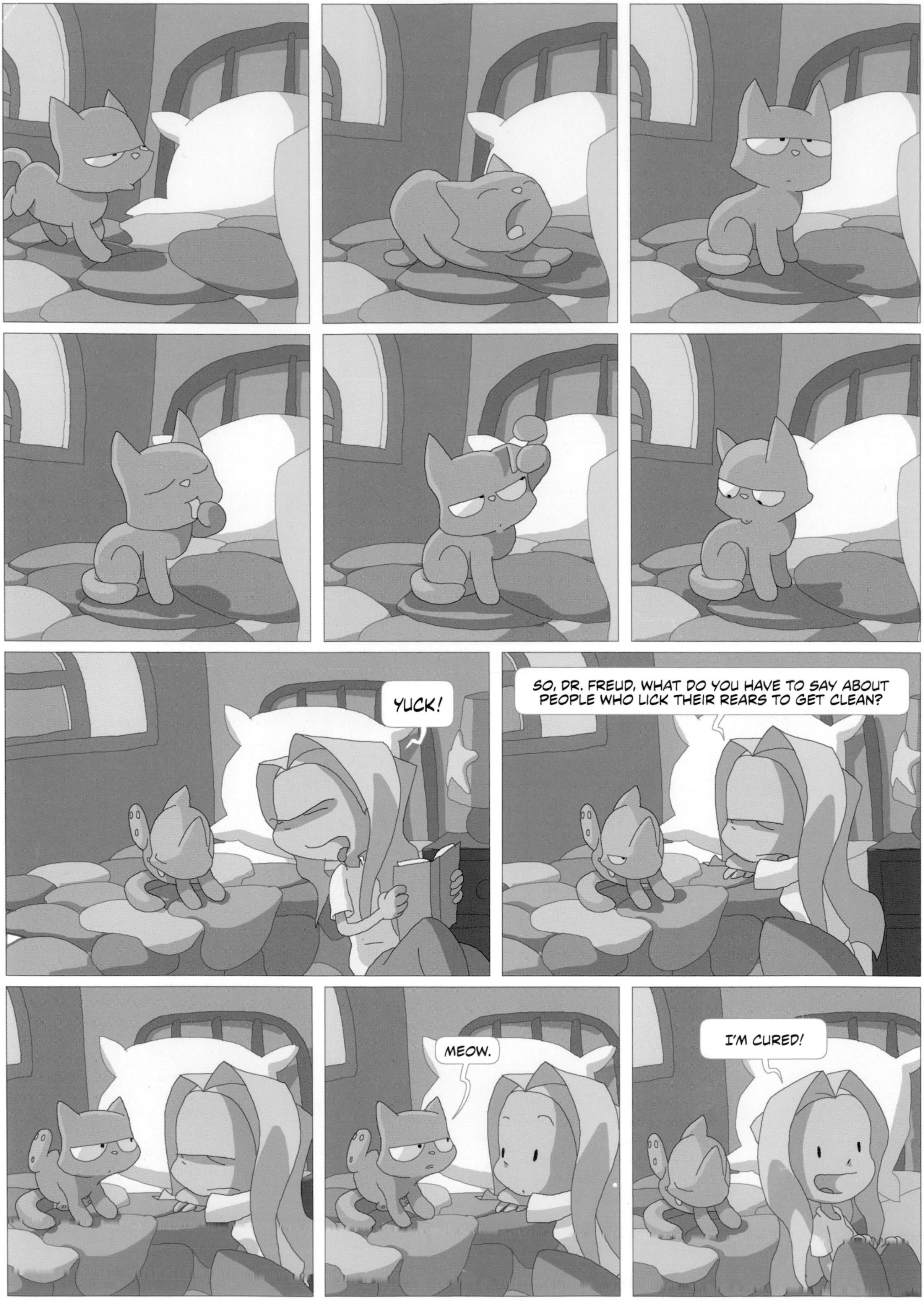
YUCK!
SO, DR. FREUD, WHAT DO YOU HAVE TO SAY ABOUT PEOPLE WHO LICK THEIR REARS TO GET CLEAN?
MEOW.
I'M CURED!

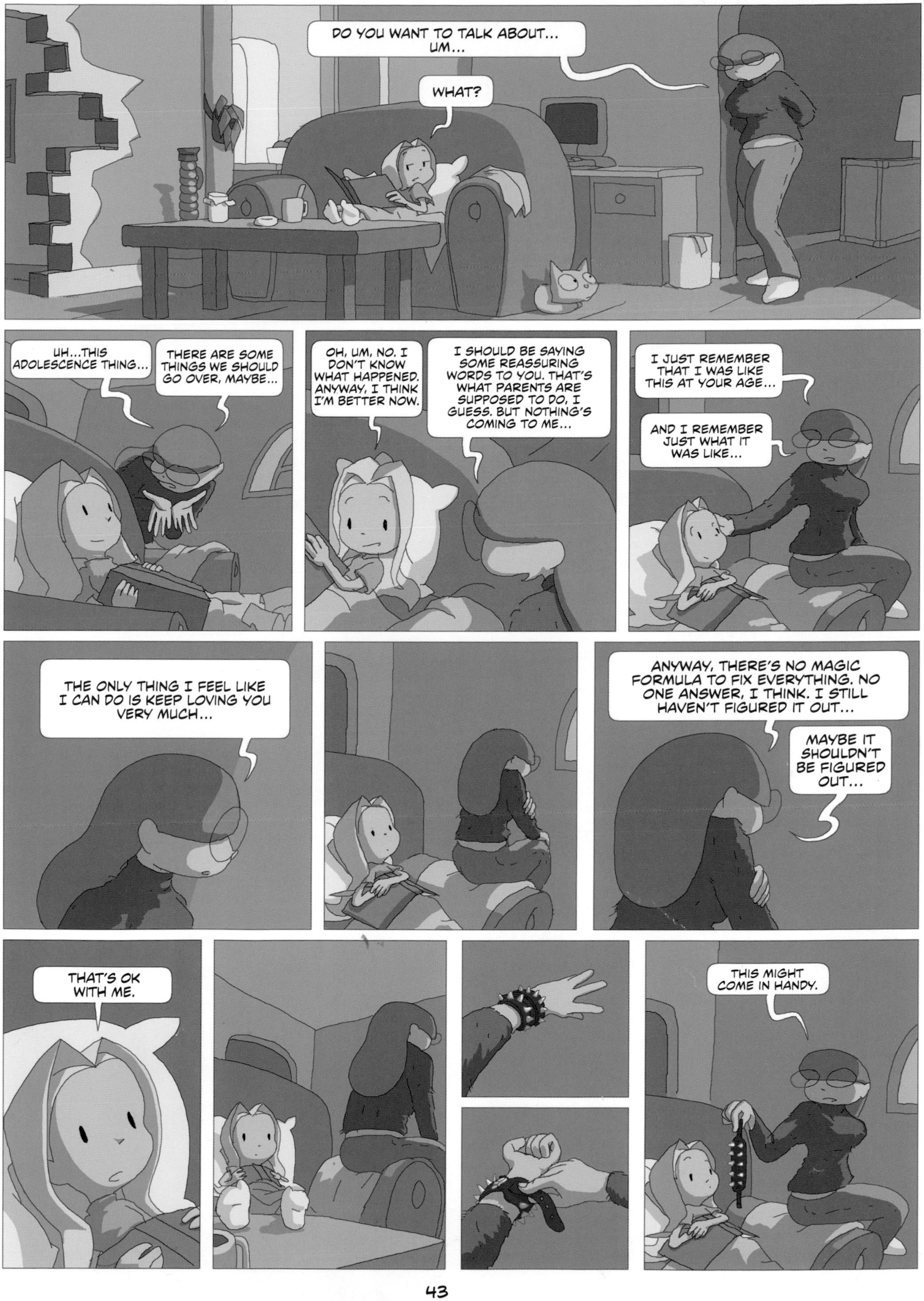
DO YOU WANT TO TALK ABOUT... UM...
WHAT?
UH...THIS ADOLESCENCE THING...
THERE ARE SOME THINGS WE SHOULD GO OVER, MAYBE...
OH, UM, NO. I DON'T KNOW WHAT HAPPENED. ANYWAY, I THINK I'M BETTER NOW.
I SHOULD BE SAYING SOME REASSURING WORDS TO YOU. THAT'S WHAT PARENTS ARE SUPPOSED TO DO, I GUESS. BUT NOTHING'S COMING TO ME...
I JUST REMEMBER THAT I WAS LIKE THIS AT YOUR AGE...
AND I REMEMBER JUST WHAT IT WAS LIKE...
THE ONLY THING I FEEL LIKE I CAN DO IS KEEP LOVING YOU VERY MUCH...
ANYWAY, THERE'S NO MAGIC FORMULA TO FIX EVERYTHING. NO ONE ANSWER, I THINK. I STILL HAVEN'T FIGURED IT OUT...
MAYBE IT SHOULDN'T BE FIGURED OUT...
THAT'S OK WITH ME.
THIS MIGHT COME IN HANDY.

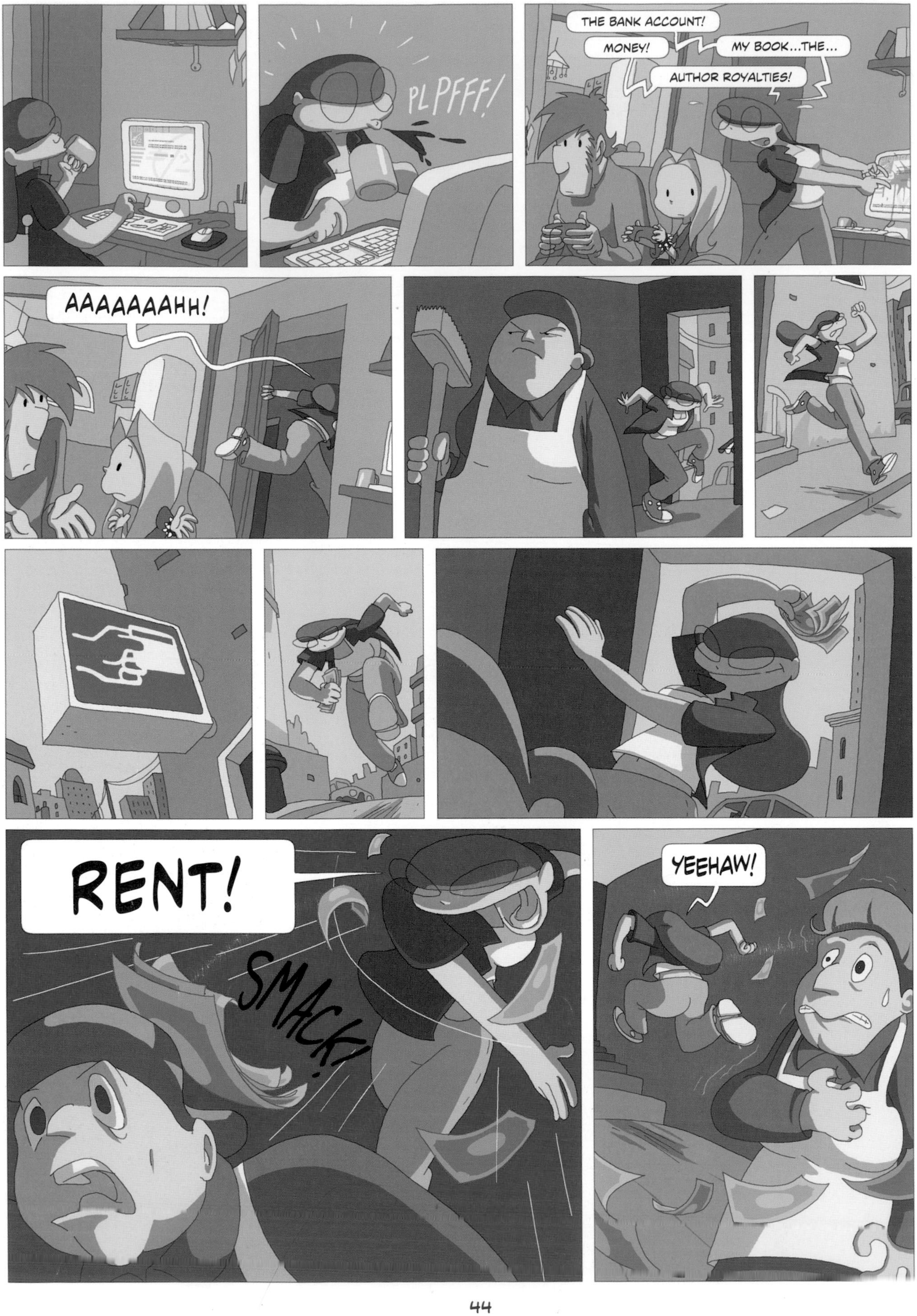
PLPFFF!
THE BANK ACCOUNT!
MONEY!
MY BOOK...THE...
AUTHOR ROYALTIES!
AAAAAAAHH!
RENT!
SMACK!
YEEHAW!

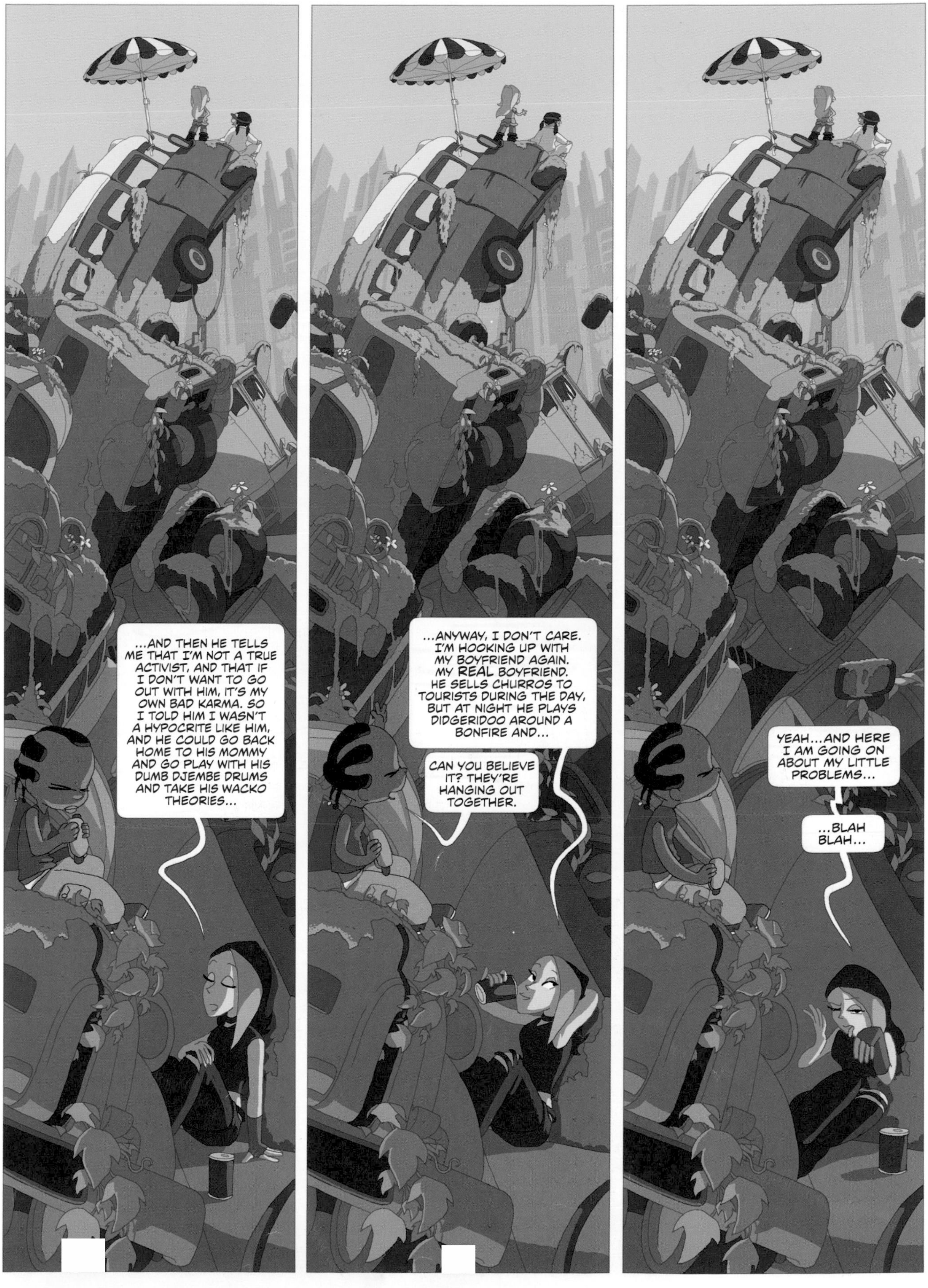
...AND THEN HE TELLS ME THAT I'M NOT A TRUE ACTIVIST, AND THAT IF I DON'T WANT TO GO OUT WITH HIM, IT'S MY OWN BAD KARMA. SO I TOLD HIM I WASN'T A HYPOCRITE LIKE HIM, AND HE COULD GO BACK HOME TO HIS MOMMY AND GO PLAY WITH HIS DUMB DJEMBE DRUMS AND TAKE HIS WACKO THEORIES...
...ANYWAY, I DON'T CARE. I'M HOOKING UP WITH MY BOYFRIEND AGAIN. MY REAL BOYFRIEND. HE SELLS CHURROS TO TOURISTS DURING THE DAY, BUT AT NIGHT HE PLAYS DIDGERIDOO AROUND A BONFIRE AND...
CAN YOU BELIEVE IT? THEY'RE HANGING OUT TOGETHER.
YEAH...AND HERE I AM GOING ON ABOUT MY LITTLE PROBLEMS...
...BLAH BLAH...

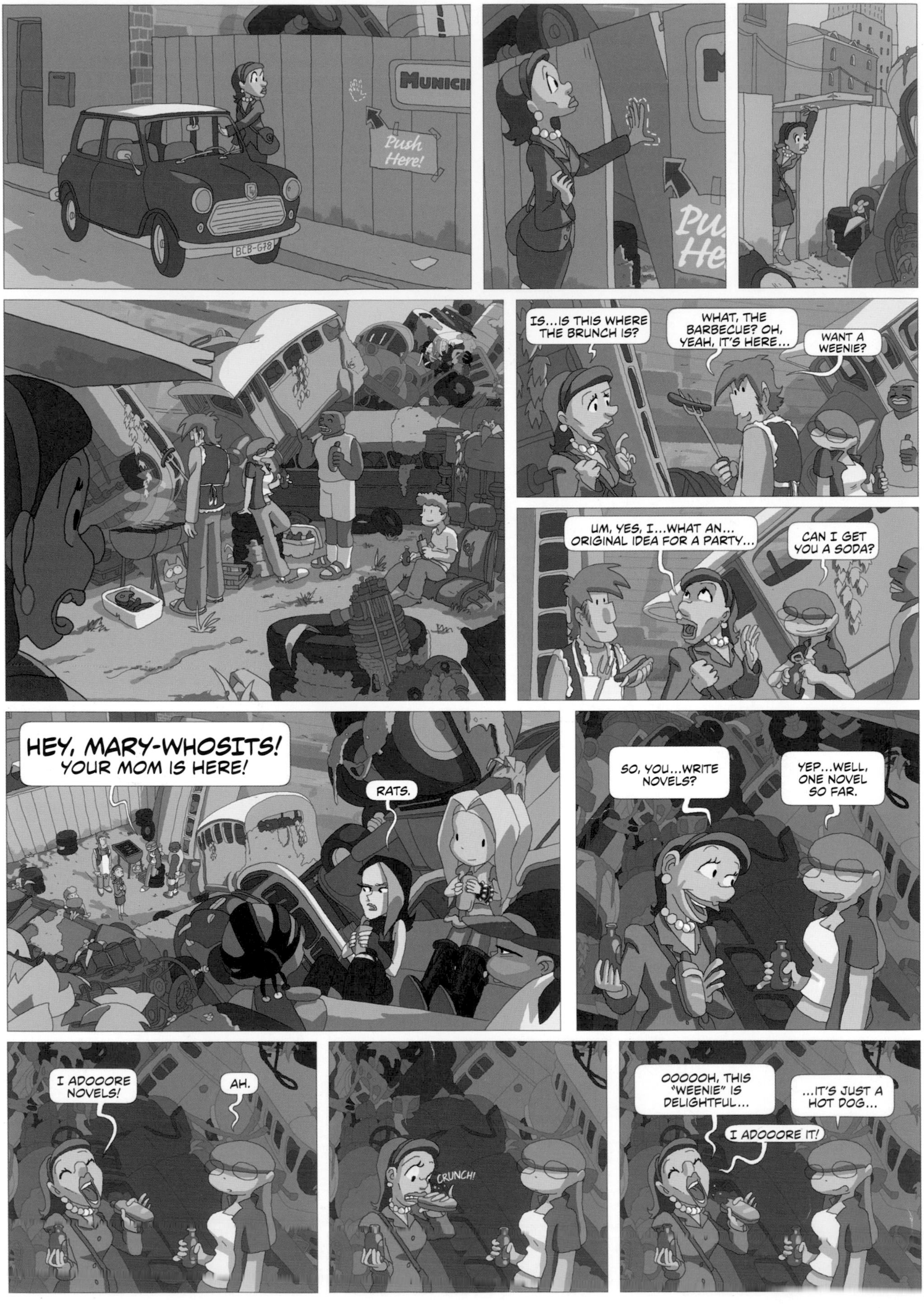
MUNICI
Push Here!
Pu He
BCB-G78
IS...IS THIS WHERE THE BRUNCH IS?
WHAT, THE BARBECUE? OH, YEAH, IT'S HERE...
WANT A WEENIE?
UM, YES, I...WHAT AN... ORIGINAL IDEA FOR A PARTY...
CAN I GET YOU A SODA?
HEY, MARY-WHOSITS! YOUR MOM IS HERE!
RATS.
SO, YOU...WRITE NOVELS?
YEP...WELL, ONE NOVEL SO FAR.
I ADOOORE NOVELS!
AH.
CRUNCH!
OOOOOH, THIS "WEENIE" IS DELIGHTFUL...
...IT'S JUST A HOT DOG...
I ADOOORE IT!

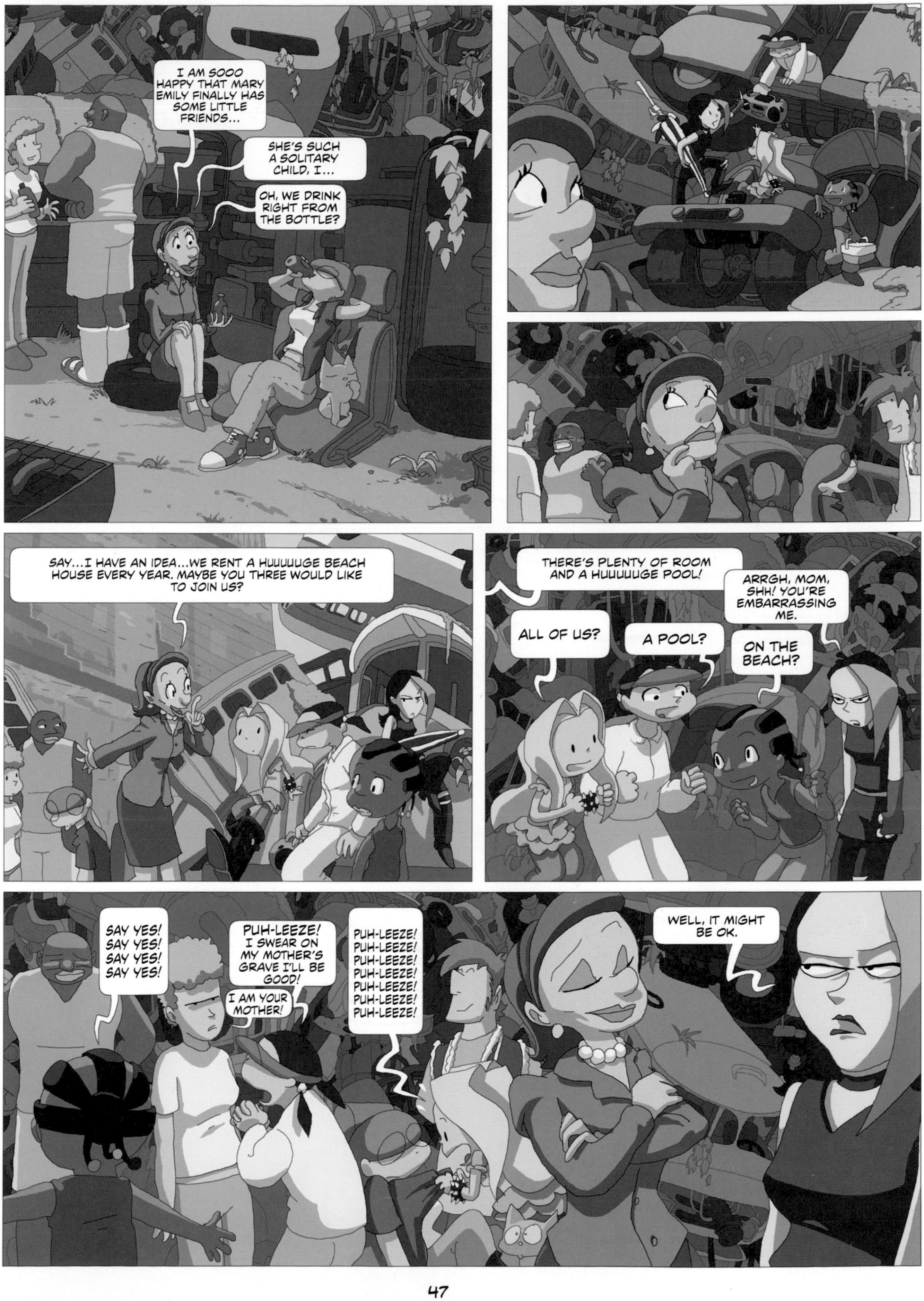
I AM SOOO HAPPY THAT MARY EMILY FINALLY HAS SOME LITTLE FRIENDS...
SHE'S SUCH A SOLITARY CHILD, I...
OH, WE DRINK RIGHT FROM THE BOTTLE?
SAY...I HAVE AN IDEA...WE RENT A HUUUUUGE BEACH HOUSE EVERY YEAR. MAYBE YOU THREE WOULD LIKE TO JOIN US?
THERE'S PLENTY OF ROOM AND A HUUUUUGE POOL!
ARRGH, MOM, SHH! YOU'RE EMBARRASSING ME.
ALL OF US?
A POOL?
ON THE BEACH?
SAY YES! SAY YES! SAY YES! SAY YES!
PUH-LEEZE! I SWEAR ON MY MOTHER'S GRAVE I'LL BE GOOD!
I AM YOUR MOTHER!
PUH-LEEZE! PUH-LEEZE! PUH-LEEZE! PUH-LEEZE! PUH-LEEZE! PUH-LEEZE! PUH-LEEZE! PUH-LEEZE! PUH-LEEZE!
WELL, IT MIGHT BE OK.

PUH-LEEZE! PUH-LEEZE! PUH-LEEZE! PUH-LEEZE! PUH-LEEZE! PUH-LEEZE!

HOLD ON. I DON'T KNOW... I WAS GOING TO TRAVEL AROUND AND DO SOME BOOK SIGNINGS THIS SUMMER--

PUH-LEEZE! PUH-LEEZE! PUH-LEEZE! PUH-LEEZE! PUH-LEEZE! PUH-LEEZE!

WE'LL SEE... IT'LL DEPEND ON HOW GOOD A CASE YOU MAKE FOR--

PUH-LEEZE! PUH-LEEZE! PUH-LEEZE! PUH-LEEZE! PUH-LEEZE! PUH-LEEZE! PUH-LEEZE! PUH-LEEZE! PUH-LEEZE!

OK, OK, BUT

YAHOO!!

WOOHOO!

HEHE!

WHAT?

NOTHING.

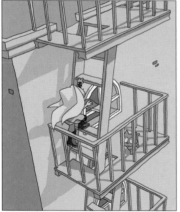

CLIC!

DEAR PAUL...

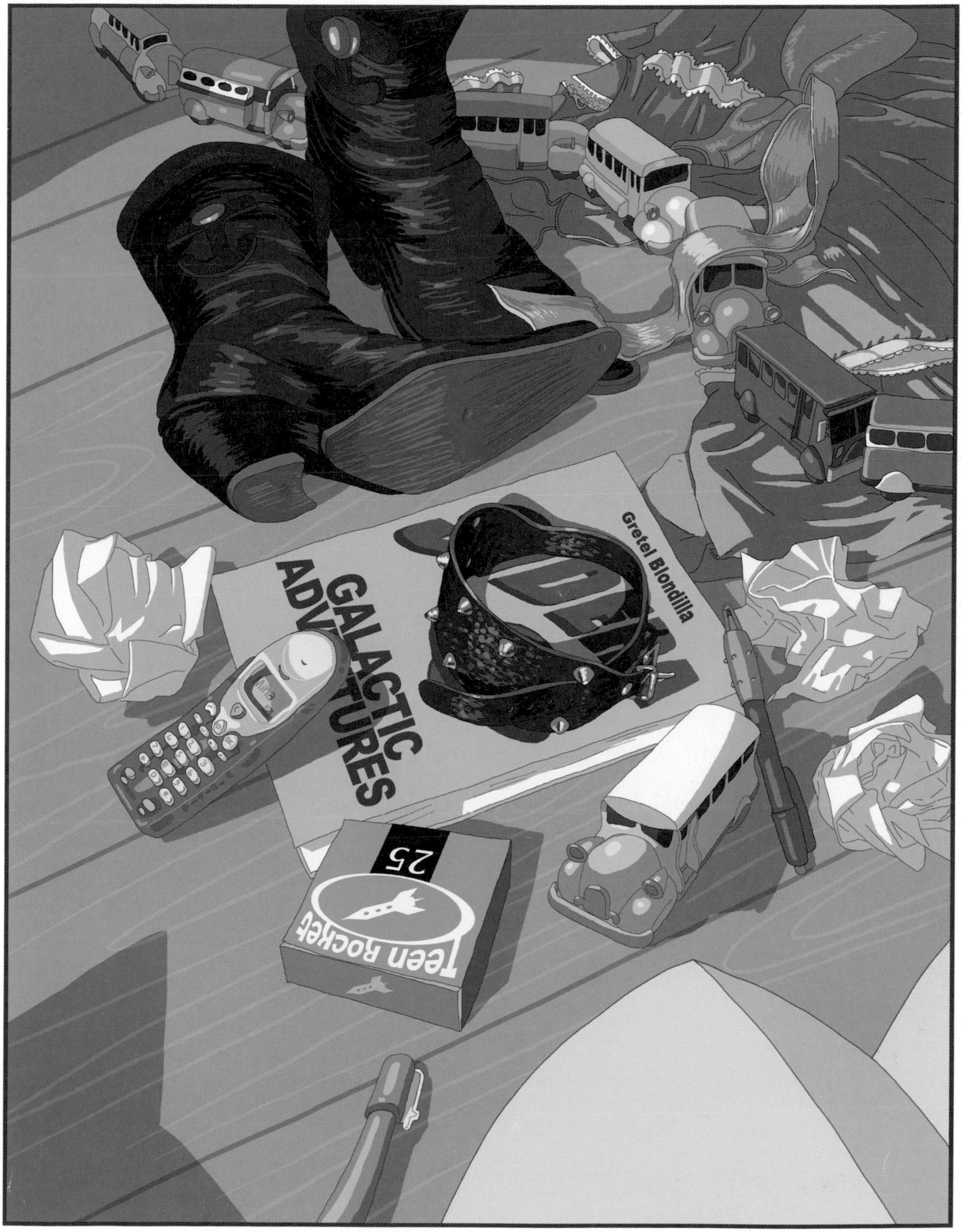

Gretel Blondilla
GALACTIC ADVENTURES
25
Teen Rocket

The original back cover of the French edition

mAry EMily

Mary Emily is a girl with REALLY BIG problems. For example, her room is so huge that, this one time, she got lost in it.

YEAH, IT'S LIKE, YOU KNOW...

STICK IT TO THE MAN, YOU KNOW.

NOTE: Actually, she's really fun. It's just that, sometimes, you have to tell her:

SHUT UP!

and after that, she's normal for a few hours.

Actually this look means: "Somebody love me, please."

KAReN

At first, Karen and me didn't exactly hit it off.
But in the end, we had a good talk and...well, now she's a friend.

So, in any case, it'd be in our best interests to get along, them, Mina, and me, since we're going on VACATION together this summer!

I CAN'T WAIT!

A sensible girl is hidden under that tracksuit. Any idea how to find her?